BAD NEWS

HOLT,
RINEHART
AND WINSTON

New York
Chicago
San Francisco

BAD
NEWS

BY PAUL SPIKE

Published simultaneously in Canada by Holt, Rinehart and Winston of Canada, Limited

Library of Congress Catalog Card Number: 70-138883

Designed by Carl Weiss

SBN: 03-085970-0
Printed in the United States of America

First Edition

Sections of this book were previously published in the following magazines:
"Box 456" in the September, 1968 issue of *Evergreen Review;* "A.B. Dick" and "The Conference Man" in the Winter, 1969 and Spring, 1970 issues of *Columbia Review;* "The Diary of Noel Wells" in the Spring, 1969 issue of *Columbia Review* and in an anthology, *A Cinch, Amazing Works from the Columbia Review,* published by Columbia University Press, Winter, 1970. "Multi" in No. 47, 1969 and "Specks Saga" in No. 49, 1970 issues of *The Paris Review;* "A Good Revolution" in *New American Review,* No. 11, 1971

TO
MY FATHER

CONTENTS

BAD NEWS

BAD
NEWS

It was a wonderful morning to leave Germany. And it was my thirty-fourth birthday. I collect tickets. Together with my brother and the engineer, I keep the Train of Thought running from Vienna to Los Angeles.

Clickety-clack, I was splashing freezing water on my face. Outside, above the soft mown hay and the lowland villages, the sky beamed with a haze called light. We were six minutes ahead of schedule. I was thinking of my wife in her blue nightie, reading a potboiler on the side of the bed. My little man was restless inside my shorts. What was the dream I couldn't remember? I missed the boys too. I even missed Long Island.

Most passengers were still asleep as I passed through second-class. I was on my way to see old Ronald, the Negro steward, in the club car. He is just about my best friend, or was, on the train. When the lights were lowered and only a few plastered gentlemen dozed in the green velvet armchairs, he would come and sit with me. First with hemming and mumbles, like a pitcher in his windup, Ronald would begin one of his lies. Perhaps his stories were true, but it was unlikely for he seemed to enjoy them too much. I think he stitched them together from other men's lies he overheard at the bar and from things he got out of the magazines he was always reading. My favorite was the one about his days training horses at the County Fair in Illinois. But there were others: one about New York City, the one about driving a famous Jewish banker around Denver. Ronald was a little monkey. Marlon Kandrac called him "boy" to his face sometimes and this always upset me. Ronald is in his late sixties.

I guess I'm a liberal. Anyway, Ronald was mixing up a pitcher of Bloody Marys for two priests who were already sitting at the bar. I guess they were used to getting up early to say mass. I said hello to everyone and pretended to check a frayed window shade as if it were very important. The company doesn't care if the window shades are frayed. But I did, I think. I care about a lot of things a lot. And this has always gotten me into trouble. First with my parents, then with my school, and finally with the little wife and the company.

I went back into the kitchen behind the bar and found some orange juice and a couple of bags of cashew nuts, what I like for breakfast. Ronald came in with a newspaper.

"You seen this, Felix?"

"What's new?"

"Look there on the headlines," he said. It read in big black figures: "Ape Pack Strikes Glasgow!" In the smaller type, it went on to explain that clans of giant apes had been emerging from Loch Ness and were invading Scotland and northern England. These apes walked right out of the bottom of the Loch. But what was most peculiar about these monkeys was what they liked to eat. They ate nothing but pound notes or dollar bills, actually any kind of printed money. They were insatiable for money. I checked the paper and it was the morning edition of the *Times,* which is thrown on board as we pass through Munich.

"This is unbelievable," I said.

"I know it! It's a joke these fathers give me. They had this paper printed up at some penny arcade back in Vienna."

"We certainly did not! Conductor, this man won't believe us when we say that we found this document in the W.C. just a few moments ago. Father Craig found it. It appears to be God's honest truth."

"You sound Irish, Father."

"I am Irish."

"Well, I'm American and I guess I don't know all that much about Great Britain and such. But do you believe this ape business? Eating money and running out of Loch Ness?"

"I say, it could be a cruel hoax, couldn't it?"

"I remember when I was up in Buffalo once," Ronald

began, "way back 1934. There was a circus performing up to those parts. Couple giraffes and a black bear run off and escape. They run all over separate, I mean several, blocks of Buffalo and the bear got hold of one of the giraffes and ate the critter. Finally, the cops came and shot him with shotguns. They got the big-necks out in Brockport later that night." Ronald was launched into one of his stories and the language was tangling around his tongue a bit.

"Do you know if the engineer knows about this, Ronald?"

"I don't know if the boss knows. I haven't seen him yet."

"Perhaps I'd better go up and show it to him."

"Indeed, indeed you had, my son. It's your natural right and obligation to do so." He was still drunk, this puffy old priest. I bet that he was one of those they call the Benedictines, but as I wasn't Catholic I couldn't tell. In any case, I went straight to the engine. My brother Rudy was up front steering the train, but I found Marlon cutting breakfast sausage at the table in the engineer's mess. He was looking sharp in his scarlet jumpsuit with the company insignia on the breast and the white boots coming up to his knees. By nightfall, he would be soaked in crusty oil. But his face was pink this morning.

"How are we doing, Marlon?"

"Six minutes ahead, as you damn well know yourself, Mr. Conductor."

"Right."

"How are the skirts on this trip?"

"Nothing too spectacular."

"Nothing like that floozy in the first-class last week?"

"Marlon, I wonder if you heard about this crisis in the British Isles yet?"

"Nope, I ain't heard nothing about it."

"Seems there is an invasion of killer-apes all over Ireland, I mean Scotland. They come walking out of the Loch Ness in groups all the time and they are running berserk across the countryside."

"Who do you think you're talking to, Felix?"

"I just read it. Some monks found the paper back in the toilets. Apparently, these apes eat money. They attack banks and stores and run up to people on the streets and chomp right through their jackets to get at a wallet full of bills."

"That's a little hard to take, Felix."

"It's the truth."

"But it could be some kind of new demonstration."

"What do you mean?"

"It could be some kind of protest march. Or one of these political shutdowns. You know, like the kind of stunt they had with the burning dollar bills in the Stock Exchange, you showed me once?"

"That was in New York."

"Still, it could be these goddamn hippies."

"That is possible."

"Sure, these hippies are crazy. They could have put on skin-diving gear and then ape suits. Then run around eating each other's money."

"They eat other people's money."

"Even more likely!"

"I don't know. I don't figure this. I don't see that these hippies have ever had enough guts to work and this takes a lot of work. They throw flowers. They throw bags of urine. But I don't figure they have the guts to risk a felony like bank-robbing."

"That's a twenty-year sentence."

"Right."

"But these college students are crazy enough to do it. They would rob banks, sure! They burn banks. Why not rob them? I figure maybe they're getting a little smarter in their old age."

"Well, it could be that this newspaper *is* a joke. Somebody might have left it in the toilets to spook these priests."

"Are you sure these are real priests, Felix?"

"They drink like fish and their socks smell, so I figure they are."

"These British are all eccentric, you know that."

"Yeah. Maybe you ought to radio up ahead to London, though, just in case. We could use the real information on this."

"Hell no."

"No?'

"Hell no. I'm not going to call and ask about apes eating money, running around Scotland in their underwear or something. My pension is due in less then ten months. If you want real information, you call. Go ahead if you want, but not me."

"I don't know." I didn't relish the prospect of Bert

Whitehead teasing me about this for the next two years. But I was curious. And I guessed it was my obligation too. So I went into the tiny radio room and called Bert. He said it was definitely true.

London was dark and it smelled. It smelled like wet dirt. We were stalled for some forty minutes before they told us the trip was canceled. I spent the next hour advising the passengers and supervising the clean-up crew. Finally, I got out and walked through the great network of cranes and engines in the yard over to the tower. Marlon and my brother were drinking coffee with Bert Whitehead.

"Happy birthday!" said Bert when I walked in. The others screamed and laughed. I figured they would be drunk by this time. The coffee was actually whiskey.

"Happy birthday, you giant dollar-bill-eating gorilla!" yelled Marlon. He had his shoes off and it was not very nice.

I sat and they pushed over another mug and Bert poured some Teacher's into it. There was the latest edition of the paper and I read it. Apparently the apes were spreading out from the crowded areas and creating sanctuaries up in the moors. Five people had been killed in events connected with their attack, though not one of the deaths was directly attributed to the apes. Mostly it was soldiers who got caught in their own cross fire. One infant had burned when a jet crashed into the side of the house it was sleeping in, up in a town called Sayberry. The papers said that all communication with the ape-infested areas was restricted by the government. No roads were open up North either. They were calling the apes Red Mandrils because apparently they had a reddish fur. I hadn't noticed it, but I drank the whiskey in three big gulps. This whole business made me shiver a little. And Marlon's feet were stinking.

It was pitch black as we headed out through the main gate. We went directly to Willoughby's, where the railroad men always stay. There were plenty of rooms. My brother and I shared one up on the third floor, but it took me a long time to finally fall asleep. The room was very stuffy. And then a woman began to scream somewhere in the hotel. A sudden impulse told me that she was being raped, and I threw on my pants and ran into the hall. But then I could hear better and she sounded like a drunk. I got back in the cold bed, and finally, long after the first nauseating rays of light had flooded the room, I dozed.

I dreamed of Vera, my wife. It was in the parking lot of our local shopping center. She was selling raffle tickets with two of her friends at a card table. I walked down into the lot and suddenly I saw a big car with a clown in the front seat. It was my father. He had been dead for three years at the time. But in the dream he was still alive and he wanted to talk.

I can't remember a damn thing he said.

"Right now," said my brother. He was shaking me awake. "So let's go." Marlon was already waiting for us downstairs, finishing his coffee, which he said tasted like "shank oil." We crossed the big avenue and walked back through the main gate of the yard.

Mr. Gunner came out of his office and told the three of us to come in and have a seat. He was a short man with a brown mustache and a baggy blue suit that was all wrinkled where he sat down. I had difficulty looking at him so I looked at my brother instead. He was magnificent in his company uniform, a scarlet jumpsuit.

"How do you feel, men?"

"Never better in all my life," said Marlon, who was always the first to brown an executive.

"Well, I'm sorry about all this. I've just finished talking to New York on the phone. They have the latest news from Scotland and this time it is the truth. The newspapers in Europe are all censored and all wrong. This scare about the money-mad apes is rubbish. Complete fabrication. And that is no accident, boys. It is a clever cover story for the real truth. What's been going on down here is nonsense but what's going on up there is worse. I can't give you any details because they couldn't tell me much. But it is frightening, terrifying, and a tremendous tragedy."

"What, sir?" I asked.

"There has been an enormous accident in Scotland. It is spreading. That's really all that I have been told. Something involving our massive technological gadgetry or whatever. Apparently, people have been ignoring things and ignoring things until things themselves decided to ignore people. The result may be a massive wipe-out." He took a handkerchief out of his pocket and blew his nose loudly.

"Is this a train wreck, Mr. Gunner?" asked Marlon.

| 11 |

"Among other things. But just as a consequence. You boys know what your government and ours has been trying to do over the last decade?"

Nobody said anything.

"Neither do I. But whatever happened was a sort of revenge. There are no facts. The military is going berserk, shooting up the people, crashing into each other, they they can't find an enemy to plaster."

"Is this something involving atomic energy?" asked my brother.

"Nothing. No rockets, no lollapaloozas. It is strictly a natural catastrophe and it is affecting the people greatly. This is some kind of natural correction of some monstrous error on the part of some monstrous nobody. We seem to have run out of enemies. That is why I can't even begin to explain this to you."

"Holy Jesus!"

"Even Holy Jesus won't take the blame for this one, Mr. Kandrac. Of course, you are all sworn to secrecy on this until you leave England. And now the bad news for you."

"What's left?" asked Marlon

"I'm afraid the Train is going back to Vienna with a skeleton crew. The company is going to have to lay you all off."

"Now wait a minute!" yelled Marlon. "What do you mean lay us off? A few months before I'm due to retire. Wait a second, Mister Gunner. The Company can't do this! This just isn't possible."

"I'm afraid that unless you are willing to go up into

the infected area, there will be no place for you men in the Company now. We are sending a few blotters and a crew of scags up North. I doubt if you would like to join them."

"How much does it pay?" I asked him.

"About a dollar a day, Felix."

"That's unbelievable," said my brother. I nodded. So did Mr. Gunner.

"You two brothers are young and should have no trouble finding something as soon as you get back to America. As for you, Marlon, I sympathize."

"This is bad news," he said.

"And I will put in my report to the Company that you ought to be allowed to work out your final months in some type of position. I will recommend it upstairs."

"What about you?" I asked him.

"I have a feeling that I'll be sacked before too long myself."

"Tell me, Mr. Gunner, is there riots up there?" asked Marlon.

"Yes."

"Then why don't they use the Army?"

"It's mainly the Army that's rioting, Marlon. The civilians are having an easier time coping with this one. It's a matter of flexibility and what people are used to. I should imagine the Army is used to having some answers."

"I can't understand this," said my brother.

There was not much left to say. Soon we left his office and picked up our checks at his secretary's desk. We got a cab outside the gate and told him to take us to the airport. "I wonder what will happen to old Ronald?" I said.

"I wonder what they'll do when they catch all the niggers who started this fire?" It was Marlon. We got to the airport and had a few warm ales and watched the big planes muck around outside in the rain. Marlon began to feel better. My brother began to cry a little, but in a very subtle way so that he thought nobody could notice. I was trying to think. What would it be like back in the United States?

SPECKS
SAGA

1 · THE RISE...

Change your thoughts and you will change your world. It's guaranteed for ninety days. You can't buy a man with a cup of coffee and a sandwich. Spread out mats for him. Offer him stools. Let the host present the cup, the guest will return it. Wash the beaker, set down the goblet. Line a colander with cheese cloth. Spoon in the cheese mixture and then fold ends of cloth over the top. Imagine the excavated dirt. Set in larger bowl, open eyes, catch any drippings.

Comfort is a surface, a straight line. The emptiness of comfort astounds man. It is like the world's most powerful ray gun.

Headache again, thought Mary Ellen, flicking out her fingers to lock the red wire into the small red terminal of the distributor casing. Then she sent it off on its way down the black rubber conveyor belt. Off to the waiting hand of her friend Claudine, who would snap the two rubber nipples into place, top and bottom, and pass it, in its turn, on to Miss Kostoy, who checked automatically for terminal imperfection before throwing it back into the flood of identification tags and parts of black plastic tractor distributors that flowed on to the runty girl who was Final Inspection, No. 1774, Sec. 07. Her early afternoon headache and as usual the break was an hour off, an hour and ten minutes. Red wire into red dot terminal, snap, replace, hand out, shut, snap, replace, snap, replace, and retrieve.

Mary Ellen in her sanitary green coverall smock has been at work only six weeks, so she is still not sure of herself, nor really one of the family here in the Mahwah plant. Drinking coffee in her room, lonely and tattered in the Dulston Hotel in Mahwah, she wonders about her loneliness and blames herself for not being friendly enough. She knows she is too shy. Afraid to talk at lunch. She only talks to Claudine, her friend. Mary Ellen likes to lie down in her slip with a cup of coffee very hot, careful not to spill, before running to the bus at seven fifteen a.m. Soft brown hair and full lips, perhaps she is too skinny. Her job pays well.

Walt used to take her to his company dances, and usually they were happy times unless he got stinking and started chasing other girls, even other men's wives, and telling her to sit in the car. I'm not taking any more nagging bullshit! And then he left. She got her divorce after seven months.

So this was Solomon Island. A Princess extension in the bedroom gives a night-long sense of security when Dad's away. "How are you sweetheart?"

"I love you."

"You're mine."

"All yours. Oceans of love and millions of kisses and may you soon be in your own home with your own husband."

"Today you got three men, none of whom had met the other previously, to talking about religion naturally and interestingly in a couple of minutes. What's your technique?"

"This is from me to you, a rich spasm. I notice you are 'straight up.' Perhaps God created it so."

"Hungarians love good food. Wet and heavy like a soggy sheet and sprinkled with a few old raisins. For example, thumb-sucking and masturbation are tension-reducing, but the former does not satisfy the hunger nor does the latter serve the cause of reproduction."

"You have found the key: by Faith you have accepted God's power and He has given you the hint you needed."

The world's most powerful ray gun. . . .

"I cannot advocate too strongly that marriages be built on spiritual foundations."

Rock of Ages. . . .

If you receive a malicious or obscene phone call: hang up! Do not keep talking. The other party may be in the middle of an orgasm. That is what the caller wants. Always, before, Nancy had played tennis with her father on Sunday mornings. He had seemed marvelously youthful to her.

Even after a hard-fought set, in the most intense heat, his sparse hair lay neatly in place and his tough face remained dry and his breathing regular.

Chris stretched out in his seat aboard the 707 and suddenly received an image from the past. From his boyhood in Rhode Island. It was of the back of his father's hardware store, where he worked after school and summers. Ah, he shut his eyes and sucked in the cool musty air and the darkness of the store, the rows of boxes and the bags of seed and fertilizer. Shelves of paint and racks of tools. And the clanging of the register. Chris had liked to work there beside his parents. He had been a hard worker, just as he was a diligent student in the local high school. He was a tall, good-looking boy with jet-black hair and flashing eyes which changed color depending on whether he was standing in the sun or the shade. They were blue in the shade and brown in the sun. He was defensive about this one deformity in his physique, and for a period of his early adolescence he walked around squinting so that no one could tell exactly what color they were. When girls asked him about his eyes, he answered, "What difference does it make?" They never asked again. They usually asked him these questions up in the hills, in his car—a beauty, it won him two prizes at custom shows.

Then Chris was awarded a full scholarship to Brown University. It was the happiest day in his parents' lives. But, after only a year and a semester there, the Dean of Students called him into his paneled office off the Quad and told him, he paused and hesitated, Chris had flunked out. Too much social life in the beer-soaked cellars of Brown's fraternities. Too much athletic enthusiasm and not enough time behind the books and in the labs. He couldn't go home, back to the store. His parents would never forgive him. He packed up and went to New York. And two weeks later his mother sent his notice of induction into the Army. And then two years later, he was back in the Big Apple, in New York. Hungry, depressed, and without the faintest notion of where he could find a job.

Recently, rioters had taken over an entire section of the country. Led by two Senators and an Epileptic, they were in complete control of Nebraska, Missouri, and Kansas. All state borders were barricaded and the rebels had confiscated for their own use a factory that was the sole source of chemical Mace in the United States. This was the property of Mr. Thaddeus Mace.

Nick Vicarion came out of the foreman's office. He was a tall man in his early fifties. His face was ridged and cut with the scars of struggle, a life of work and brawls and falling off cattle cars into luncheonette fist fights as if he were an ordinary slob but something more, a modern risk with a family to support. He drank a lot but was now a leader of the rioters, the discontented and the disconnected. He had problems. Too many punks thrill-seeking ran off into the corn fields with an aerosol spray can of knock-out gas. They thought they had found the ultimate high: unconsciousness. Coma . . . with no dreams. Just a brain full of dull neutral gas. Nick Vicarion was in charge of security around the Mace plant. His ass was in trouble, big trouble.

Pepe came to in the chill of the corn. The twilight sky was enormous in its windy isolation crow-eyes. He heard the dreams of his boyhood run behind the Mexican stove. This was the footstep coming through his empty belly. Red beans in a mush on the burnt spoon. The flies and the crabs. He raised the can, he felt his finger press the tiny plastic button and the soft whoosh. . . .

Vicarion used to be Thaddeus Mace's gardener, but now he was in rebellion. They wanted their rights. The television came out in eerie, ghost-blue light on the modern Dodge City street, empty but smashed-up Pontiacs and heel marks on the rain-damp blacktop of the A&P parking lot. Once when he was tying up a rose bush, he had been startled when a cowboy boot drove six inches up his spine, cracking his guts open in a surprise of violence and blackout. It had been old Mr. Mace. He laughed and walked on, leaving his gardener in the thorns.

Mr. Mace was an ex-Rough Rider. He shot his way up San Juan Hill beside Teddy and then up the corporate staircase, executive by executive falling before his young boots and knowledge of where and what a buck is: he knew his money. And now he was in Washington at a top-level conference in the heart chamber of the Justice Department, laying out plans for the imminent recapture of the liberated States. They decided on a simple plan. At a given signal, thousands of soldiers dressed like carnival workers would ride up the various approach highways to the captured territory. The rioters, it was well known, were in poor communication with one another. Thus, each group of people manning their individual barricades would think, "Here comes the circus!" The soldiers would smile and push into position a neon atomic calliope which would oom-pa-pa while midget riot police hopped about in pig costumes with blue lace collars. At a designated time, the calliopes, perhaps ten thousand of them, would shoot ultra low frequency sonic booms into the enemy zone. This would create a net of sonic waves, a sonic checkerboard. The frequency was set to freeze human nerve cells. Also, the victim made a mess in his pants.

Vicarion looked out over the beautiful rolling turf of America, he saw the golden ears of corn and the distant mountains like massive toys but spectacular because they were real. He thought of the movies and he thought of the sunset on the plains. Once, Indians might have set up tents on this very plateau. The neon out on Route 66 was coming to life in reds, yellows, blues, and greens. The rioters had lost. He felt this in his gut but didn't know when exactly the feeling had been born. They had asked too much. He once had been so comfortable, so happy grilling steaks and drinking dry London gin with lemon soda mixers in the hammock of his suburban house. He loved his family very much. He had been satisfied with the programs on his television. He wished he had the world's biggest ray gun for tomorrow. What would it feel like to be assassinated?

The sound of crickets out in the fields of the American farm country was crisp and every now and then mixed with the hiss of spray gas.

The professor made a motion for him to sit down beside the desk. There was a moment of silence in which they both looked at the cluttered desk. Then Eddie cleared his throat and said, "Sir, I have had personal problems this term which made it impossible for me to attend too many classes."

"Never mind, son. Does that really matter with four of our states seceding from the Union? That this nation is on the verge of destruction cannot be denied any more. This may be it! You can have your C—, that's not important. Mark my words. What is important is whether or not you youngsters are going to learn a lesson here. Realize what you have done! This is civil war!"

The first thing Chris heard was the roar of the huge jet engines dragging him through the sky, and then he realized he had been asleep. He looked at his watch; it had been a good twenty-minute nap. Her hand was warm inside his fly. Just then she was trying to maneuver his erection inside the tangle of his shorts so that she could get a firm grip on it. After an instant of grappling, this was done. Her index finger found his glans and chaffed the little mound of tissue gently. Then for a second scratched his penis with her silver-painted nail. Chris looked up at the stewardess and smiled. "What's your name?" he asked.

"Darlene."

"What difference does it make?" He ran his hand slowly up the sheen of her stocking. Slowly and smoothly over the tan silk. Until he reached the softest pillow in the world: her gorgeous thigh, bare and rounded and up above the tight silk panties stretched over the damp blonde mount of the goddess Venus, whom nobody believed in any more.

He poked a finger under the thin crease of elastic and into the gush of her light groove, up to the pink bubble, wobbly as a greased marble. A pearl under his finger tip. And then he was back with Noel in her Sutton Place apartment. He had taken her out for a bite of supper after the movie and then walked her across the fanfare of the East Side and up to her place. She invited him up for a nightcap and he had accepted, eagerly, she thought, and smiled to herself. Chris was sitting on the edge of the couch when Noel came out of the kitchen with the two highballs in her hands. She gave him his rye and ginger and took a healthy sip from her own vodka and Coke. Then, suddenly, without any warning, she was on her knees before him with her hands clutching his ankles and her face burrowing in his groin through the thin material of his summer trousers.

"I want you more than anything. I need you, Chris," she moaned to his penis. He was taken aback. It had happened so suddenly. He took another sip of drink. Then grabbed the nape of her neck.

"I want *you*, baby!"

"Good good good, I'm so glad glad," she moaned.

In the locker room of an Idaho junior high school, twenty riot police were hanging up their clothes, counting their change, and getting into the carnival costumes. Tons of muscular lard with red splotches on their thighs and great knit underpants, perfumed feet, and teeth as clean as jewels, they joked about what a handcuff across the knuckles could do to someone's eyeball.

As we saw the police rip into the demonstrators, tearing clumps of hair from pretty heads and beating boys to their knees, where they filled their mouths with steel-capped boots, we began to shout and to set up a chant: Mace Must Go, Mace Must Go, Mace Must Go! I found myself in this mob shouting a different slogan, one which was not taken up by more than two or three others: Mace Must Die, Mace Must Die! We knew there was a difference in slogans and that words made slogans into the world's most powerful thighs. I lay down on top of the language and found myself entering an interior universe, hung with adjectives, and clustered on the floor were the colorful nouns. I found enough for a sentence and then. . . .

She had his long dong out and was resting for a moment on her haunches, smiling at its bulbous head stuffed with hot stuff. She leaned forward and gave it a lick, then another, then ten more. Then she slowly took the tip, big as an orange, into her straining wet lips. She had a full mouth and she shut her eyes. She sucked.

The traffic came across town in a flash flood of honking horns, and then white doves, one million little feathers, swung into the lagoon. He knew the buzzing in his organ. Electric wires spelling BINGO on the steps of his nervous cathedral, the back brain, and then the flash of thick come in her throat. It was splashy with salted almonds, and she swallowed twenty hungry times, opened her eyes, looked up, and grinned at him, his penis still in the pink gap of her throat. She said, "Let's go in the bedroom."

Material comfort is simply a beginning. A mark it has taken us millions of years to *take*. Man needs a context beyond comfort. We need a group consciousness, the consciousness we left behind in the ocean, in the jungle, and in the huts. The world will eventually become one planet-village. We will be primitive once more, for all men will be ignorant of morality again, all men will share the same interior tools. Eventually, it will be unnecessary for man to work. Eventually, it will not be possible for man to work.

But creation will continue: the creation of beauty and of time.

What time is it? wondered Chris as he stepped out of his trousers. Noel was already naked and waited across the dark in her Hollywood bed. He could hear the traffic on Sutton Place. He could hear the soft plink-plink as Noel brushed the lint from between her toes with a finger nail. He dropped his shorts and tiptoed to the bed. "What time is it?" he asked as he gathered her cold flesh in his arms.

"Are you as worried about these riots as I am, Chris?" He could not answer, so he concentrated on the sound of his nerve cells as they splashed against the ceiling of his sexual receptors.

"Noel, I think these riots are the worst thing that ever happened to our country, save, perhaps, for the Civil War and the assassination of all our greatest leaders. These riots, this lawlessness, makes me sick to be an American. Young people today know no better. I'm not surprised, the way they have been brought up: 'ethical culture,' baby books, et al. But the adults, they're the ones who I just can't find it in my heart to understand. They make me want to cry sometimes. I don't want even to talk about it any more. Let us go to sleep, okay?"

"I love you, Chris. You're the best." He thought about this and concluded she meant "in bed."

Chris imagined he could almost feel balmy air inside his pressurized cabin, thousands of feet up. But he knew it was a silly fantasy. For some reason, he suddenly thought of Holbach. He was a Newtonian who believed science explained the world and that there was no need for a first cause. Chris believed deeply, with all his heart, in the non-existence of any first cause. That's why we can have all these jazz masses. Chris liked Holbach for not believing in first causes. He hated the philosopher named Ricardo, the man responsible for the Iron Law of Wages. Just then, before he could visualize all the poor people doomed by Ricardo to starvation and venereal disease, the wings dipped and the big craft fell back to earth.

2 · ...AND FALL

She is sitting in a white string shift, her back to the bay and a smile flickering, as he walks up the dock. Tall as a Watusi, she seems. Dark brown hair flowing long, a rich mane crossing the small elegant bust. A face which is deadpan and wealth and front page, definitely front page. Chris nods to this stranger and finds a seat on another bench. They are waiting for the boat that will carry them across the mile or so of dancing blue water to Cole's Island. My first vacation in three years, Chris thinks. The sun is beginning to boil the atmosphere into a tight grease. He has trouble keeping his eyes open in the glare. The island looks too scraggly and thin in the distance. He has heard so much about the place. Will he make out all right over there? He wonders, scratches his face, fingers his tennis shoe. He glances at this towering beauty. Her legs are ivory, long shapely tusks. Her hips are too thin for him, perhaps. He likes a tight aristocratic ass, but this is too tight, almost too aristocratic. He moves his eyes up to inspect her. . . .

"Do you like my breasts? Or do you find them too diminutive for your taste?" She speaks very crisp with the dry ice and needles of a Back Bay girl. Radcliffe?

"Excuse me." Chris is abashed.

"I mean, buster, how do you like your tits? Melons or hardballs?"

"Excuse me. Did you think I was looking at you or something?"

"Of course, and why not? Actually, you look like a hardball man. You can almost see my nipples through this string thing. Nice, huh? I paid my ass for it. You better believe it, those chi-chi Village shops."

"My name is Chris Richards."

"I am Manda d'Cours Vermillion Vaugir. Are you a guest of Cole's too?"

"Afraid not. I've got a room at the New Collision."

"Ghastly place!"

"They tell me Cole is quite a host. Is that true what *Time* said about his parties, Miss Vaugir?"

"Bet on it if you want, darling, I never know what to believe about the little fatman. He's quite a host. If *Time* says it, it's true. Kiss me?"

They talked and laughed their way across the bay, and when they reached the other side Manda invited Chris to come up to Cole's hotel. She got into a yellow bikini while he looked around her terrace, and then she led him down to the private beach, a perfect crescent set into a lush little hill. The trees were full of parrots, and servants ran up and down the shaded paths in white jackets carrying trays full of pastel drinks.

"But I don't want to join the firm, Dad. And don't tell me one more time, please just don't keep repeating. . . ."

"Don, do you *know* what it's like not to have all the breaks? You have enough food, enough clothing and shelter and money, and a good background and a degree from Princeton. These are some terrific breaks, Don. Now you want to throw them away? I've spent my whole life trying to make you people comfortable."

"That's just it. What does that mean, comfort? What does it mean to be relaxed and comfortable when millions of people are starving?"

"They don't have your breaks, Don."

"Listen to him, Donny."

"Mom, Dad, can't you understand that comfort means nothing to me?"

"If you go limp, cocksucker, I'll kill you!"

"Send in the fifty-four mortars to perimeter three. Give Don's squad a back-up. Let Willy hold the flank and Moroni will put a tail on the arrow."

"Can't we just be friends?"

"The assassin was apprehended at 0650 hours. . . ."

"I saw it!"

"Oh yeah sure! tell me ha ha ha tell me again about your 'truth' and 'beauty' baloney. Those are just your wild notions, Don. Wait until you have some family of your own. What do you know, frankly? I'm fifty-two years old and I've done. . . ."

He met the elderly professor on his way to the bar. "Hello, Dr. Banner. How are you this evening?"

"Fine, Willy, fine. On your way over to the Tiger Inn? I'll walk with you, if I may." They decided to have a pitcher of beer and found a booth toward the rear of the darkened tavern. Groups of students were clustered at every table, some singing, some talking, one boy in an absurd hat reeling in some solitary revel from table to table, the waitresses dodging him as they delivered their pitchers of beer.

"What did he say then, Don?" He explained his father's anger and ignorance to the man.

"Now listen, Don. Of course your father isn't too anxious or even capable of giving up his personal vision of life. He will probably never reach such a point. My advice—I know you are going to moan—is try and compromise with your parents as much as possible. At least while you are living at home."

The waiter brought him a Silver Star in an iced sterling mug, and Chris reclined back into his rattan beach chair. Manda's bikini was astonishingly erotic. The material was thin and metallic, extremely clinging. He could just imagine what her mount of Venus must look like, yet he could only imagine this through an imaginery net of yellow material strung across the front of his cortex. The beach was fine and white; it brought the word "emerald" to a spot just behind Chris's lips. The mystery was like that of an air mattress in the vacuum of the sunshine.

"Are you feeling it?" she asked.

"What exactly?"

"My charisma . . . your drink . . . the expensive sunshine and the overdose of vitahealth trickling through your short hairs, what do you think?"

"What are we going to do about dinner?" Manda laughed as the waiter brought another round to their table. Chris was turning drunken somersaults above the white sand.

"Let's finish these drinks and then decide."

"Okay by me," she said and took a healthy swallow.

Don faced his father across the mediation table. "I'll give you the railroads from Long Island to Rochester, Calcutta to Bombay, Minsk to Istanbul. Also increased wage benefits for hotbox specialists and for caterers." Don removed a felt-tipped pen from his breast pocket and awaited his father's reply.

"Son, I cannot accept that offer. Honestly, are you serious? I want some peace here. I want total disarmament and a hot line set up from Washington, Paris, and Rio directly to Peking. The Israelis will have to defer to our council, at least for a few more years."

"Sure, fine. But right now I'm trying to pin down this transpo section, Dad."

"Calcutta has an epidemic and the guerrillas won't pump out the Pittsburgh enclave for months, which directly affects all of the East Coast. How about this submarine highway in the Pacific?"

"You agreed to leave that route for Russia, a token perhaps, they'll go for it. The American government will iron that out."

"I want to keep this in the family, you know that, Don."

"Look, Dad, what about railroad ticket concessions in

college towns? Do you want that as well as the heliport and the Nigerian mines?"

"Sis can have the Rose Bowl and we'll give your mother the parade."

It was dark and the sky was full of silver pins by the time Manda took drunken Chris by the hand and led him up the white gravel path to her room. They decided to have dinner on her terrace, and Chris took a long, steaming shower to melt the alcohol out of his system.

As it touched the lunar ringular probe, its nosecone retracted into a concave "dwelling" position. The specks seemed to come in patterns reminiscent of the structure of molecular music. We have our feelers in Decode hampering the decoders into a sitting position.

They lowered their tariffs after two days of the idiocy. Everyone recognizes their action as typical of the Eskimo mind.

Whom would you choose? The Eskimo or the Eskimo-like Indian? How about if they wanted to be your valet? Or just dry your back? Or touch your fish with their bare hands?

The idiocy was mirrored in her pills.

Belgium crashed today!

Brussels in agony of poverty! Hungary sends aid! Eskimos sending fish. U.S.A. pledges "investigation."

Manda insisted on taking Chris to the nightclub owned by Cole Klein: the El Gitano. It was located on another small private island, reachable only by one of Klein's private launches.

The first thing Chris noticed inside the place was that

he was freezing. His hands felt blue. Klein had installed the finest air-conditioners in the world, custom-built in Germany, designed by his own Japanese engineers. It was very cold and very dark. Red lumia light flickered on genuine English oak walls. The club had three stories. The Watchtower Room was the first floor: gypsy dancers, flaming steaks, and strictly for the tourists. The "Cave" was located one floor down and was a romantic underwater dance floor. Finally, in an elevator in the Cave, you could descend to "Cole's Heaven": strictly members only, the most exclusive room for five hundred miles.

Manda pointed him out, a tiny fat man with a red face and a dome who squinted through radium shades and was wearing an olive Universe Blazer designed by Jaime de la Hunky of Alicante and London.

Dark conversation and another round please! Another round pumped into Bolivia caviar insects climbing out of rotting democracy specks . . . just like the bandits to take this jeep . . . and make it "straight up."

The Benson children always spent the Fourth of July watching their daddy light Roman candles in the vacant lot in Union City. The night Mr. Benson saw lines on his tongue twisted the fire-stick in the soul food his shit hole his armpit the children screaming from behind the glaze hurry up, hurry up daddy, let's go to the vacant lot!

Jim came into the tent and laid his rifle down. He lay down on the blanket. His breath was roaring, full of choking gasps. A streak of jungle grease across his cheek. Morris came in.

"That was a close one! Charlie almost had us with those 54's down by Pien Tup until those Mustangs buzzed in. You feeling okay, Jim?"

"My penis is buzzing."

"Er . . . you want me to call the Sarge or Doc?"

"No."

"You thirsty? Want some water?" He offered him his canteen.

"No. What would you think I want, Morris? No, forget that question."

"Sure thing, Jimbo, sure thing." He went hunting through his pack for some chocolate.

Cole comes bobbing across the room toward Manda and Chris.

"Well well well. Hello Manda darling dahling girl. Who's the penis?"

"Cole Klein I'd like you to meet Chris Richards. Chris is a hardball man and my latest escort, also I think he's not wealthy."

"Nice fella, nice fella." Cole begins to pick up empty glasses in a mockery of his bondage slaves imported directly from Capetown to service his club and hotel.

"Nigger, oh Nigger, COME CLEAN THIS TABLE!" he shouts toward the kitchen. Then he turns to the blasé yet nervous Mr. Stu, his maître d'hôtel. "Give Miss Vaugir and her date this table, all right, Stu?"

"Certainly." He clicks wrists and presents menus.

I cannot accept the nomination.

"The pleasure is mine."

Cole leaves on another tour of his room, stopping at

each table for two or three nice minutes of money talk, mopping his brow with an orange saffron handkerchief. He never orders a drink and the house rule is: No Free Ones. After thirty minutes, he's back at their table.

"What's that you drinking, Chris fella?"

"Red Eye, your native specialty, Mr. Klein."

"You like to fuck, Chris?"

"Er . . . sure, of course, as much as anybody. More, probably."

"We don't allow enthusiasm in here, son. Now hear this: don't fuck with Manda. She's a whore. A whore who only fucks for prestige and trades in men for shopping carts and the right mascara."

"Oh, Cole, you must be kidding, you little millionaire."

"Excuse me, Mr. Klein. Don't you care for Miss Vaugir?"

"You want a hot tip?"

"Not another joke, Cole darling," sighs Manda.

"Buy Music. Forget cold securities and watch out for oil. The assassination has changed everything. The fix is in. Buy Music. That's it, straight from the Big Boy, now you two dance or something. . . ." He fades off into little candles and red linen tablecloths.

"Wow, he's something!"

"He's right, you know. Buy Music, you'll make a killing." She took his hand and led him out onto the sparkling marble.

Mr. Cosgrave was standing beside his camper when he first heard the shadow of a rumble. He looked up to Old

Baldy but saw nothing. An auditory hallucination? This vacation had been a hallucination. He continued to tie down the mattress with his plastic rope. Mrs. Cosgrave was washing out their breakfast dishes in the ladies' comfort station. Then he heard the second rumble, then the explosion numbers one through fifty. Crashed rocks gravel boots chipping trees into matches his teeth birds a declared emergency his body squash red stains gauze cast off.

When Chris finally suggested that they leave, Manda agreed readily. She rose and clapped for Mr. Stu. He loped across the carpet with a handful of menus.

"Why yes, Miss Vaugir?"

"Send the bill to me, Stu."

"Certainly."

The dark water of the bay lapping against the side of their cruiser was hypnotic. Manda leaned against Chris and sighed. He was staring up at the enormous full moon. The biggest he had ever seen.

"Manda, do you wonder why the stars look so good when it's hot? And why the moon seems so much bigger when you are out to sea?"

"Wasn't that squirt Cole just horrible?" she replied.

"I suppose so."

"Chris, would you make love to me tonight, now, this very night?" She ran her hand up his thigh to his penis, which immediately focused. Her other hand around his waist and massaged his sharp coccyx.

"You can make me so happy, lover boy." Chris then went fumbling for her clitoris in a pile of garter belt, slip, skirt, and panties. "I'm rather well-dressed," she giggled. They did not notice the boatman photographing them with his infrared flashcube for Cole's collection.

The point is not to radicalize a small group, but rather to politicize an entire population and then the entire human race. Then it simply becomes a cycle of de-politicalization and re-politicalization. This will keep the hungry happy, while the scientists can get us farther into space. The computer went dead with a leafy tube sputtering in static rings. Isn't this Wednesday? said the editor. He made a blue mark and thought a little about changing the world.

The computer changed the soap for the men. Jim came into the room with his hands full of circuits. He dropped a tungsten prophylactic gauge, the duplication boys screeched and ran to him, tackling him around the neck and dragging him toward the giant E-series 7077. He went to sit down.

The newest conflict in Asia as reported to the negotiators. He lay down as he stood up as he tried to smile the tears filled up his hands as he started to stare at them his eyes had already been dead ten seconds.

Chris got his socks off. He glanced across the terrace. Manda was naked. He stared at the glowing white of her rear. She was staring wistfully over the darkened salamander of Cole's Island. He went to her and took her in his arms. The wind drove a cool moisture into their embrace. She shivered and turned her cruel cat's teeth into his lips, a canyon of low roar somewhere down her throat.

Over and over the waves of desire pounded on their fictional bodies, the limitless darkness plunging in a swarm of phallic references and grunting rhetoric. They made love like drugstore sex, like cardboard. So full were they of their one dimension! Over and across the linoleum of the luncheonette they rolled, knocking over a rack of paperbacks, grinding their loins together in a pile of 95-cent readers, the slick centerfolds of the place dancing to some inner knowledge, finally, then, after the paper trash of their phoney orgasm, Manda farted and looked up at her man.

The tape left in Chris's hotel room follows:

SPIKE: Chris, what was your nickname in high school?

CHRIS: Move your pencil.

SPIKE: Why?

CHRIS: Is this all an elaborate way of getting me to fix you up with girls?

SPIKE: Have you ever felt the Siberian winter lace up your ribs in a perfect scream?

CHRIS: I would like to talk by myself now. You, so far, have been moving your pencil, or pressing your keys, some writing procedure, until you have arrived at exactly this spot.

SPIKE: No, I haven't arrived anywhere. That's the funny part of the illusion.

CHRIS: What?

SPIKE: The funny part is the illusion itself. The serious part is behind that—the illusion's control. Its energy and its creator.

CHRIS: You wrote the story.

SPIKE: Wrong, at this moment I am writing the story. I know that in my memory. I do it in the present, in the electricity of my cells, right on this stupid dot.

CHRIS: The period. Now I would prefer to return either to the religious experience I have had recently or to some of the sexual episodes earlier on, some of that fine oral sex.

SPIKE: Sorry, but you have to help me decide a serious question.

CHRIS: You mean, "Is the Novel Dead?"

SPIKE: Certainly you can say that. It means nothing. It's not dead certainly and on the other hand it was hardly ever really a living organism. It is sort of a parasite resting in the flux between you and me, in the illusion's energy.

CHRIS: I would like some of that fucking back soon. Even in words, fucking is better than anything else.

SPIKE: That's one point: of view. Which is lost in a maze of points. Fucking is good, that is a point. If the novel is dead or not dead, that is a piece of nonsense useful only to chew around in the ceremony of the classroom. To discuss its "death" is certainly not even a "practice" let alone a point.

CHRIS: I would like to say that the specks have begun to rage in my chest, four hundred New Yorkers falling down . . . neutrinos corpses dust bullets hit rotting democracy specks and new words, each word a bit of new ink, each linked into sad dashboards across the page, a holy child.

SPIKE: Each holy child is indeed a new word. But the question, the question. I need your help in formulating the best question.

CHRIS: What is it?

SPIKE: That's the problem.

CHRIS: That was a question.

SPIKE: How do you feel?

CHRIS: A long distance in my flesh. I feel like a fool with a youth attached. Something to wear money on, to send children into institutions, into battle with some steel and some little wit. I feel like you move your pencil.

SPIKE: The problem is: you can feel. I can feel you feel. The problem is there is a bomb here made out of left-overs.

CHRIS: I have nothing to do.

SPIKE: Right.

CHRIS: But there is something here.

This ends tape.

Chris did not hear his own voice when he came onto the tape. He was in the shower, singing a little song to himself, washing the crud off his tired body and feeling better. Then the character of Chris is played by No One In Particular. The character of Mr. Mace was played by a bitter load of vibrations carried in specks from one vibration pack to another, like wild, foaming dogs let loose on their own graves, spitting up tokens and passing in exchange. The character of Noel was played by A Girl In Particular. The character of the Oriental bartender was played by A Nation. The character of No One In Particular was played by the almighty Will.

BOX 456

Dear Miss Box 456,

I want you to know that I don't make a habit of answering ads like yours in the *Enquirer*. Not only that but I never even read the paper. But this morning I found a copy on the seat next to me on the bus I take to the office and decided to just look through it since there wasn't anything else to do except just look out the window. I take that bus every morning. And I noticed your ad while perusing the classifieds. For some reason I have been thinking about it all day and finally have decided that there is nothing wrong with writing this letter even though I know nothing is going to come of it probably.

I am thirty-four and 6′1″ with brown hair and eyes. My build is lanky, still good from the athletics of high school days where I was varsity basketball. Right now I have a good job with the city here. This is as a route delayer on the Albany Power Company. You say you are twenty-nine years. I think the age difference between us is just right for a normal relationship between adults. Also I like "chicness, vamp eyes, and girlish figure" as you claim to have in your ad. I am a mature guy and self-supporting as you ask for.

You also claim you want "sensitivity." I am this. For one thing, I read a lot. My usual reading matter is books by Will Durant and *Profiles in Courage* by our late President John F. Kennedy. I am sensitive, I think, because though I don't have many problems of any nature I am lonely sometimes. As you know, it is very bad to be lonely in this day of many population explosions. I also try hard to understand the problems of my friends at work. They can get into some tough scrapes.

You say you have been married once. I am not concerned whether it was divorce which split you apart. Please write and tell me your name. I would also be interested in a photograph of yourself if you have any handy. If you don't write, I will understand because these things are pretty stupid. I do admit I wondered what kind you must be to place an ad like this in a filthy paper, but I can understand since sometimes people get very very lonely. Write.

Sincerely yours,
Wallace Coombs

Box 456

BALTIMORE, MD.
JUNE 12, 1966

Sister,

Your heart, your broken heart, has called out to me through the pityfull yellow pages of the *Enquirer*. You are walking with the wrong company (the DEVIL!) through your own valley of pain and tribulation. BUT we are praying for you. I am walking beside you, Sister, every pathetic step you take in your sin.

Especially is JESUS CHRIST, the SON OF GOD!

I trust we are of the commen faith of Christendom. The sickness that has caused you to place an ad in the newspaper for the purpose of oral-gentile contact can be healed! With JESUS!

Enclosed find two pamphlets I have authored. I am praying for you on my knees sister!

Keep a chin up for Jesus,
F. Bob Silvestor

NEW YORK CITY
JUNE 12, 1966

My Dear Miss Anonymous,

When I read your advertisement this morning I felt perhaps here was the soundest investment of all, the girl of my hopes and dreams.

I have just retired from a prestigious brokerage firm

where I held a status position for a good many years. Since then I have been looking for the perfect retirement bonus—a girl with those "vamp eyes and girlish figure" you promise. Bachelor life has turned to dust in my eyes, and I seek the tenderness of womanly companionship which I can lay upon with all my worldly goods and my unspent reservoir of filial affection.

My interests (aside from women) are high finance, naturally, fine arts and vintage wines, and a good round of polo. From my window, my living room window (my apartment has three and a half spacious airy rooms with good light), you can get a view of New York which will practically take your eyes away. Not to mention my car, a Ferrari! This year's model. If you could forward me a photograph of yourself, perhaps one in a swimsuit, I would so appreciate the gesture. I look forward to our first rendezvous, with open arms.

Yours,
John T. Tolchek

BROOKLINE, MASS.
JUNE 12, 1966

Box 456

I lay wake dreaming about your big pussy all night. My cock ten hard inches. You dig 69? Send picture and number so I can come fuck you.

Tobbler Lugo

P.S. I give you best lay you ever had. Best in universe.

Box 456

NEW HAVEN, CONN.
JUNE 12, 1966

Dear Miss

As a senior at Yale University, I am engaged in a special research project. I would like to ask you a set of computer-selected questions concerning your life as a single, middle-aged woman in contemporary American culture. I hope you will be interested in my proposal.

Since it is summer, I would be free to meet you at any time convenient to yourself. I am busy working to save money for next fall's tuition. Boston, New Haven, or New York would be quite convenient meeting places. What is the most convenient for yourself? Of course, there would be an honorarium for this interview. Perhaps fifteen to twenty dollars. One last request, a photograph would be an especially welcome addition to my records. Please reply as soon as possible for there is a deadline to this project. Thank you again.

Sincerely,
Donald Gold

BERDOM, OHIO
JUNE 12, 1966

Dear Miss,

I hope soon to have your name and perhaps a photo of you. I hope you see fit to comply with my letter. I am no stranger to this kind of introduction through the U.S. mail. But, so far, no luck in finding the right woman for me. My name is Roy Miller. Yes, I am interested in full-time marriage.

I am forty-one years old and grew up on a farm in Iowa but have lived in Ohio for over twenty years. I guess I had just about as happy a childhood as one could ask for without being the son of a rich oil millionaire or something along those lines. When I was twenty I got hitched to a beautiful girl. We had been sweethearts for a long time. At the time I was with a trucking company since my older brother tom got the farm when Dad died. My wife and I moved to Toledo when I was twenty-two. I went to work on auto bodies and now am foreman of that same shop. I live out here rather than Toledo itself. Two years ago my wife Berta left me with another man. I have thought of murder but can't find them. Are you divorced?

I work hard but have some hobbies. I watch TV, mostly sports, play some cards, don't drink to get drunk, and don't speed in the car. During Christmas I build cute little toys out of metal for the children of my close friends. I am mature and sensitive. I am proud of the way I handle myself in a tough situation and don't usually end up an emotional mess.

I hope you are a good cook and housekeeper and don't mind my smoking occasional cigars at times. One more thing, I believe a wife should be spanked at least twice a week in order to make her more humble and respect-

Box 456

ful to her husband. I will use my hand and sometimes a hairbrush on your bare buttocks. Write soon please.

Yours truly,
Roy

BOGOTA, N.J.
JUNE 15, 1966

Dear Mr. Lugo,

Frankly, though your letter began on a rather sharp note, I was soon overcome by its charm and found it gratifying in its honesty. Believe me, that is a rare quality in today's troubled world. My phone is 331-7220. Call as soon as you can. Will send my photo under separate cover.

Love,
Brenda Orlando

P.S. That would be nice.

A.B.
DICK

The worst day of the year. At 5:00 A.M., a thick storm pasted itself across the sky. Beneath it dragged a hundred wild winds like brass chains. Cornices were lost in up-drafts and broken trees spread like crazy.

A.B. Dick didn't even have a decent coat. His thick wool overcoat had been delivered for annual cleaning just a day before the great blow. By the time he got to his first appointment, cereal and juice, he was a cold towel upon some wire bones. Or wet to the root. It was luck that he wandered into the bar and happened into Frag-state who was soluble but drunk. Fraggy bought him a double whiskey to soften the onset of this miserable eve-ning. He seemed on the verge of eruption into destruction except for the thin emerald scarf tied Indian-style around his head.

"Ay! And did you spy the two creatures yonder, Mr. Dick?" asked the plastered gentleman.

"That crowd?" replied A.B.

"You poetics give me a royal pain," said Fraggy.

"Do you know them?"

"In a pig's eye. Do you want them yourself? A lick fit for arhh. . . ."

Fraggy fell back straight off his stool and onto his head which smiled in a narrow crack at the base of the sky and where unconsciousness planned to stay for some time. The blood was pouring and a mess. A.B. watched Julio, the fat pear, attempt to collect the flood with a yellow broom, thin eddies of red fluid crissing and crossing the old tile floor. Fragstate's blood was hardly steaming. Dick knocked back the dregs of whiskey with a certain swift elan and plodded over his cosmic friend to the door.

One two, hup two and around the corner, down the slope, and arrive at number forty-eight, apartment forty. Ring the bell. Soon enough a quick and angry buzzing unlatches the door, itself hung with curtains sadly ruffled and de-beautified with soot. A.B. went to the mailboxes. He peered at the names. On he passed to the elevators but it was blighted. He turned for the staircase and nearly bashed an old lady very intent on discarding her sopping bag of rinds and cellophane egg driggings. Dick politely skidded aside, lost in his mind.

The apartment door was painted a deep undistinguishable color. At eye level there was a circle of mirror, a protective device: "one-way" to keep out the undesirables. A.B. leaned closer. Beneath it was stuck a piece of yellow paper with some scrawl. "Janet, Marlie, and Jean." It was an intrigue now. He let fly the doorbell. And again.

"Who's there?"

"Hello! My name is A.B. Dick and I've come for my books. Are they still there?"

"Just sec"; sounds of a police lock flew through the door like iron flappings and scrapes. Many months before he had lived in this place. But only for two days. When he left, the owner had kindly allowed him to store his library of books in the rear closet. Now the owner was gone and the apartment had recently been acquired by Janet, Marlie, and Jean. From within came hilarious sounds of gut-shaking laughter, fierce, womanly snorts.

"How do you do?" She collapsed a bit in hilarity. Then bucked up for another try. "We wondered what kept you, if you were ever going to come?" Then she fell back into another hysterical fit.

"What's so funny?"

"There's no joke," she said, and bit her lip so that a baby tear rose in her eye. "Nothing's so funny. Forgive me. We have your books. Come in, please."

"Which are you? Janet? Marlie or Jean?" He had crossed the threshold. His hands ticked away in his pockets now. A pink rash surfaced lightly across the top of his pectorals.

"I am Marlie. Now please, just wait a sec while I see if the coast is clear." She turned to see too late a bra-andpantied stranger collided in her face. The stranger squealed and flew into her room, the door banged shut. Marlie smiled while Dick was a little more bewildered. An imaginary tidal wave of female laughter crushed him to his knees here in this hallway and demanded some kind of terrible absolution for some long forgotten social error. Perhaps he had some dirty books?

"Where are they?"

"What?" She looked hurt.

"I mean, I hope they haven't been in your way."

"No trouble. I keep them in here." She motioned him into frilly territory. A blue bedspread covered with stuffed doggies and curlers and lotion bottles spread across all shelves and then there was a desk with a black high-intensity lamp beating down upon some blank yellow paper. A legal brief lay to one side.

"Are you a lawyer?" he asked.

"No, but it's one of my interests. My father was a judge. In upper New York State. How do you like my room?"

"Very nice."

"Could you explain something to me?" she said and he turned to receive. Three ways of waking up:

a) A gong is attached to the foot of his bed.

b) The door slides back. Big Chang enters and begins his slow, steamy dance. Breathing slowly in the fog, the mountain girls ease the pajama pants off your feet. You have nothing to worry about. After all, Big Chang goes back to his cage. The draining commences.

c) She has a kiss waiting for Tony. He flexes involuntarily.

Three approaches for Marlie:

a) Remind her of the cottage days. Of her sister's birth and the thin, black "garta" snakes. Tell her again of man's inhumanity to man.

b) Show her your inner being. Let the good times roll over you in a vast burning sensation along every line. Repeat together: "This is the most unforgettable week." In a Chicago accent say, "How much for this frigidaire?"

c) Cast the first stone.

Marlie climbed out of bed and put on her white rayon slip. She kneeled in front of the bookcase while A.B. wondered if he would be able to sleep. She ran her finger across the spine of each book until she found it. It was a large brown volume: Clorox's *Formal Behavior and Judeo-Christian Mores*.

"So that's what you were laughing about," said A.B. He stretched his arms in wing position and could feel the satiny coverlet beneath his wrists, cool and smooth.

"Well, you have to admit it is a filthy way of looking at things. I had heard of this book but certainly never knew it really existed." She came over to grin at his naked body.

"I don't have to admit anything, Miss Marlie. What are you looking at?"

"Your bod."

"What for?"

"Just curious. It's cute. The peenie too."

"What are your roommates thinking?"

"They can think anything. That's not true. Who cares anyway, since they're both horney as toads." She reached down and tweaked his navel, which was a bit of an "outie" and the cause of much youthful concern to Mr. Dick. "It's cute, too," she said and climbed aboard his broad tub of belly to ride him like a plow horse though he only shut his eyes and thought secretly of how he was going to get out of this idiot's clutches.

"I feel better than I have in months," he lied. His body was grinning quietly though.

"You trying to figure out how to ditch out from here? I'll bet your are." She leaned down to punctuate with a bite that stung his soft shoulder and made him think of bashing her head into the wall.

"Of course not." He felt this Marlie trying to drive the top of her head through his sagging stomach and reached out to flop a wallop on the back of her head. She groaned playfully and rubbed his skin with her brunette strands.

"Why did you think Clorox was dirty?"

"I didn't say he was dirty. It was his way of seeing things that was filthy. His perception was positively vile." She licked a ribbon of coldness up his whiskered neck and sniffed around his lips. "You smell like a little booze."

"I had a drink earlier." He was trying to remember Clorox's thesis. Something about the reversibility of responsibility. Were these girls overly religious?

"You drink so early? You bum."

"Stupid. A friend of mine was in the bar and he's in rather serious difficulties these days so that I couldn't refuse. I drink for social reasons and strictly out of respect." Like social diseases. He liked to watch his lies turn green and spread. She was fondling his elbow with a dull set of molars.

Fragstate recovered his vision in the middle of the corridor on the way into the emergency room at St. Machi's Clinic. He reached for the back of his head and found it three inches earlier than usual. The male nurse was not going to stand for this. Stand up for what? Fraggy couldn't hear well yet. He reached for his ear and got a club in his neck instead. The little greaser grinned and made an obscene spitting gesture in his face. Holy cow! Or was that an expression? He wondered where was A.B. Dick now. Living up to his name, he bet.

"Don't start that again."

"Don't start that again."
"Well, I'm trying to get it right, for Christ's sakes."
"You need a hand, Dr. Drysdale?"
"No, this is a lower skull cinch-up job. It's a snap. This loon must have been drunk as a lord. Go see if Gloria has that coffee yet, Ned, baby."

The snow was beginning to get stale, another day would make it into a rotten mess. He rounded the corner to the station and felt it jingle beneath his carefully drawn idea paper. If you got the subtle pleasures, you had to expect to out-subtle yourself once in awhile. Or was this wanting an easy way out? Big Chang was there before he could even set up a position-three.

There was a scratch and a knock on the door. Mr. Dick dove for the bed and crawled beneath the sheets. Marlie adjusted her straps. She opened it. "What is it, Jean?"

"There's a caller to see you. I thought you might like to know. Thank you. That is all."

"Thank you kindly, Jean. By the way, who is it?"

"Big Pete," she said and went humpf humpf until you heard the door slam shut.

"Pete, I'll be right there. Hang on," called Marlie. She slammed the door and ran to the door, she missed the bed and ran to the window, the desk opened into the door and the river collapsed in her bed. "Wake up. You've got to wake up. My sister's manager is here."

A.B. had gone under the storm due to the handful of red and gray capsules he had found in the desk while she had been in the john. He strived for common understanding through his dry lips, his spinning reel set into the cone-shaped dodgers in the roof in his head.

"Get up, crum!"

"Urp. Help. What was in that yellow tin?"

"You didn't take those, did you?"

"No."

"No, you didn't," she grabbed his leg and dragged.

"No, no help from you," he said, not landing too squarely on his rump. She was screaming somewhere in Poland.

"I just want to tell you one thing, fella. Don't mess around with the pretty little family no more. Leave this Marlie alone. She's just like my sister to me and I now manage her sister. I'm surrogate father for the whole bunch. Don't forget or it's curtains." Pete had sprouts of hair like bristles poking out of his nose. And a long scar traversing half of his beefy neck.

"You win, Pete. I'll get going. But one thing more, fella. . . ."

"Go ahead. . . ." Pete was relaxing with Marlie on his lap in the green living room of the apartment. There was a tremendous pile of newspapers under his feet and in his hand there was a small bottle of wine called "Fancy Pants Select." It was yellow with a blue label. Pete had his free hand on Marlie's head and whenever he wanted to emphasize a point he would nod her head up and down while she shut her eyes and bit the inside of her cheek.

"One thing more, Pete. The only thing I have to bomb is life itself. My grandfather told me that." There was a spell of silence. Then Pete let out a low jet plane imitation whistle, coming out of the sun to burn eyes with tracers. He nodded Marlie's head vigorously, glanced at the ceiling and then back at A.B.

"Repeat that, Mr. Man-O-Man."

"I said, 'Don't hurt her. She's going to make a fine wife for somebody. The best thing that's happened to me all day. All week!' "

"You didn't say that."

"Tell him really what you say, A.B., honey," muttered

Marlie. She had hunted eyes. Then Janet came by with her beady eyes to look in and see what the big deal was. Pete told her to scram and she frowned at him, then went off to get a phoney glass of water.

Two ways of playing ball:
  a) Regulation style.
  b) In the manner of one who indeed loves the process, not the result. This is bound for glory, so long as glory remains posthumous.

"What's that noise?" asked Pete and wiped away a yellow streak from his livid mouth.
  World War Three.

"I have gas pains," said Marlie.
  "So take one of your pills," replied Jean. Pete was gone. A.B. Dick was heaped in a knot on the floor. His face was not reminiscent of anything. Pete's empty bottle was on the couch. That guy was in a funny orbit between his client, whom he appreciated, and her sister, whom he loved. Outside the winds were creating chains of fear.
  "Maybe if I do something," said Marlie.

A GOOD REVOLUTION

"The pleasure is mine," said Billy. He was squatting on his muscular haunches in short-shorts and white sweat socks. The cries of the Ecoy bird were shrill. Billy had just shown TxuTxu, the local witch doctor, how to put on a Band-Aid. TxuTxu smiled through the gaps in his yellowed teeth and sang out into the jungle, *"Optre gom buckni ti ti chi!"*

The drums throbbed back an answer.

Billy had been here in West Lhoopville for seventeen months as a member of the Helping Hand of Jesus, a missionary outfit that specialized in young fellows just out of seminary who wanted to "see the world" a bit before settling down in some local parish. Billy had made good progress with his tribe. They were former vegetarians who had become meat-eaters back in the Twenties when the Catholic wave passed through the land. Billy was the first *"ti ti chi"* they had seen in over thirty years. His first task was to make them natural again, bring them back to the old vegetarian dietary laws.

Lois was the nurse on Billy's team. She was from Rye, New York, and tall, with one side of her face showing some giant strawberry pimples.

Dowler F. Rene leaned back in his leather chair and leafed through the report. It was a classified piece on student coalitions with the Epileptic Movement and especially the dealings of a terrorist outfit called the Helping Hand of Jesus. Miss Darlington came strutting into his office.

"Yes, Betty?"

"The mustache wax you ordered from Uruguay, sir. Here," she said and dropped the thin zinc tube on a pile of security clearances.

"Thanks, Betty." He grinned thinly like a cloud of cut weed floating over the Normandy graves, his guts turning in slow twists.

Dowler Rene was a trustee of EAT: Exterminate All Trouble. He thrived on climax and academic freedom; crisis was second-nature . . . nailed to the floor of his federal garage forty stories beneath his latest white paper. Betty pulled at his electric sucker; it had fastened itself to her pink belly. The latest device from Research and Development, the hearing aid had a fetish for secretarial flesh. She turned and yanked it off her and then pumped three anxiety darts into the Trustee. He was beginning to ooze yellow smoke as she dialed the Helping Hand of Jesus Regional Office.

"This is Betty at EAT, copy copy over. . . ."

"We copy. . . ."

"Have walrus uptight. Expect trustee patrol any second. Can you locate red tape? Send bandage, smokes, and anti-sucker ointment."

"Betty?"

"What?" she asked impatiently.

"We just occupied Wheeling, West Virginia!"

"Beautiful, man. . . ."

Billy saw Lois in her bra and panties standing in the stream. The bushes were very dense there and filled with the fiery Ti Ti bugs. The brown water reached up to the middle of her thighs. He saw where it was dark beneath her panties, where the black inky hairs were resting in little coils. He looked at her bra for a sign of her nipples but either they were not erect or it was one of those thick bras. He kept wondering if she would take off her clothes and bathe her naked body. That would be foolish, he thought, since this water stains so terribly. Why isn't Lois at the hospital?

"I don't know," he said.

"Are you glad that I came? Everything was boring, wasn't it?"

"What's happening at the hospital?" he asked.

TxuTxu sat around the blazing dung fire with the Chief, the War Chief, the Ti Ti Chief, and the Chief's three sons.

"When must we kill them?" asked the middle son. His father raised his hand for silence.

"You have spoken wisely but quickly, TxuTxu. You have reminded us of our responsibility to Cee, to our ancestors, and to our medicine. But tell me, how will we enforce the vegetarian laws if we kill this Billy? Only this Billy knows the new Sanitary Vegetarian Code."

All the while, the eldest son of the Chief had kept his mouth silent. Finally it was too much. Tears broke the glaze of his eyes and streamed down his onyx cheeks. He rose and left the campfire before the others. It was the girl: Lois. She was never to be his *quihairyp,* his lover. They would put her to death first. She was the woman: the white woman.

Why go on? He lay down in the lippi grass and wept and then stopped weeping and prayed to his God. He asked for a vision, and then, the lippi grass moving in hypnotic circles around his body, the animal tufts breezing in scowls and joints of night soft in tiny wet pools, he came right up into the exploding watchtower of vision.

The plains of the land beyond the green fur, the plains beyond the tribal boundaries, were all tan and then gray and then open: flocks ran like bullets in a swarm through the yellow wind. Then a signal—a spurt of gas pierced the sky from the tip of a single wild tree, it speared five hundred yards into the air. He was alone. Walking on bare feet in the clay. Holding the ritual claw at his side and the twelve-foot lance. And then the animals froze. Their legs changed into circles, solid black tubes. Their eyes sucked back into their guts. Light beamed out of their tin heads. They no longer roared nor barked nor howled at the carrion moon. They ran as if on rails, bounced clumsily over stones, and tipped into ditches. The animals ignored his spear, for their skin was tighter and shinier than its point. They made the noise of geese.

He came to on the back of his tongue.

He wanted Lois the White Nurse.

How could he measure the value of that one desire? How to sort out the moments and classify them. He wondered if there was an Iron Law of Time: some moments must always be ecstasy and others must always be the clap. If so, how to find the ecstasy moments?

Gordon was about fifty and the leader of the Detroit Epileptic Movement. He was a big man, his fists were chunks. He had a mustache and he spit hot flame through his cold gray eyes. Gordon was sitting at the head of the council table in Debby Brown's basement, the headquarters for the Epileptic guerrilla group. He had an unpleasant job tonight.

"Debby, fetch me another Coke, okay hon?" called Georgie, the Epileptics' number two man, their fine tactician. He also was a big man.

"George, what happened with them cinders?" asked Gordon, leaning over.

"Them? Me and Jackie ditched them two nights ago in the lot by Walker's Stationery."

"How is Jackie?"

"Well, Boss, to tell the truth, I just don't know."

Daisy ran up to Claudine and threw her arms around her. The two of them laughed. Daisy sat down next to the pool while Claudine went into the den to get another bottle of vodka. Daisy pronounced vodka "wodka" even though she was from southern California. She had heard some smart Jew from New York do it that way.

"You full of shit as a Christmas turkey, George!"

"Hey, what's going down here, Gordon?"

"I'm talking about them cinders and about Jackie boy. You and Jackie forgot to cover your trail on them guns too. I mean the shipment of pistols for this July. Cause they got Jackie this afternoon and your ass is hot as hell baby because I'm after you too!"

"Gordon, you must be making some kind of awful mistake here," said George and then he laughed. Laughed and laughed because he sounded just like some rat in a movie he once saw.

"Just a little bit for me," said Daisy. Claudine poured two fingers' worth. Then she turned and smiled.

Vicarion looked over the fresh vinyl and clean turf of America, he saw the . . . distant mountains.

The drums beat out an invention in riot control. Billy had been one of the soldiers dressed for months as a member of the Helping Hand of Jesus. The rioters were all just out of seminary. Their individual test scores had risen thirty points while they worked for the circus out of the charity of the Helping Hand of Vegetarians. It was going well. Thanks. Into the new enemy zone. The Woodstock Cigarettes made him freeze a vague bluish aroma like the beautiful rolling Lois spreadeagled on the golden ears of corn and thought of the movie code now under fire.

This pleasure is mine.

We going down on them mothers! he thought as he leaned in the shadow of the Afro House, a paperback book store where you could also get good soul food. He had his piece hidden in one of the empty cartons. Just then young Betty walked by, and he saw her again as she had been that night dancing on Billy's chest just before that middle-class motherfucker left to take up his basketball scholarship at State. He was going to cut that honky's head. Next time he caught sight of that boy. He heard Billy was in Africa with the Helping Hand of Jesus, that racist prick! In any case, he needed a taste and another look at Betty's ass as she strode high and tight up the aisle of the coldcut section.

In any case, Billy finally had an excuse. This time his visit to the hospital was legitimate and not just an opportunity to moon over Lois as she ran about filling prescriptions and putting hot compresses on the wounded boys, giving advice to the pregnant natives and antibiotics to the herdsmen from Yeelie Province. He swept the mosquito netting aside and there was Lois in her bra and panties.

"Excuse me." He turned to leave.

"Billy, here's your highball. Come in . . ." she whispered. He turned back to face her. In her hand was a tall glass filled with ice and dry London gin. "How did you know?"

"It was no secret. All these months . . . in this jungle, O Billy!" she moaned, stepping out of her panties so he could see the inky hairs running in a triangle down under the nub of her body.

Billy opened his eyes. Lois was asleep on his shoulder. They were outside the tent in tall lippi grass. Billy reached out and pulled a handful of the bluish weed from the ground. Deftly, he shredded the vegetation until he had enough to fill a battered old pipe he always wore in his shirt pocket. He produced a butane lighter and lit up. The first draw was agony. The second went down like sand on fire. Then the third was . . . by that time penis with her silverpang out and resting up on the water shelf with iced tongs sinking in delicate swirls or red, red sonic viewfinders bashing his flashcube into the bulbous head. Softly, big as an orange, Lois took her bra and flash floods. He reached for the delicate lagoon. There for a soda the little pupils parading whining jet ultras for she sticks her elegant manicure up his penis. Silk panties stretched over thick come in her throat, her face an orange tent burning in the Arabian kitchen of icicle hooks bent into the aluminum gown. He signed the bill and gave each sponsor a pen. It took eleven hundred pens.

He was coming down. The consciousness walked across the jungle saying, "A pearl, a beginning!" We will eventually become "one" in some twelve-year-old's love poems.

They eventually got Nick Vicarion on the fourth day. He was on the floor of a Chinese laundry underneath a giant pile of towels. The three plainclothesmen were enraged.

"Go limp you cocksucker and I'll kill you!" shouted the sergeant who had a teflon truncheon and a belt full of anxiety darts. He grabbed Nick's hair and yanked. Nick screamed but was quickly silenced when another shoved the butt of his tommygun into the bridge of his nose. Nick was screaming in his mind, I'm a father I'm a father today no I mean I'm a father how can they do this to me I mean I father daddy help your daddy me help father help me I mean . . . .

They dragged him out to the car, and one got in the driver's seat while the two younger ones jumped into the back with Nick. As soon as they were off, one cop grabbed a green anxiety dart and stabbed it deep into Nick's breast. He took another dart and scratched a bloody line up his face. The paranoia and nameless box-cars hit the ghost in isolation lungs he screamed Nick screamed like he had an underwater underwear net choking him into another hurt he was uptight tighter than the newest metal.

The roof was very dark and cool. Juanita stepped quickly from the light in the doorway to where Carlos stood. He was staring down into the street. He took her hand and squeezed it as she came to his side. It was August in East Harlem.

"*¿Como esta?*" he whispered. She smiled slightly and kissed him on the lips, leaving a trace of cool moisture there like a drop of sun condensed into pretty sweet water on the rocks of Vermont.

"I love you, Carlos."

"Quieres tu tambien, para siempre, Juanita."

Electron Eve was the fourth Tuesday in August. On this night, the nation gathered before their screens and sat mesmerized for four-and-a-half hours as Mr. President threw barrage after barrage of changes into their living rooms. He sat in his blue suit and bulletproof Mr. President mask while the nation's children grew uneasy, whining and bickering until their parents had to tranquilize them and send them to bed. His speech was called the State of the States Address. Much of it was devoted to changing people's addresses: "Mr. and Mrs. Marlon Kandrac will move from 18 Pleasant Way, Nombe, Utah, to West Twenty-first Street, Newark, New Jersey. . . . Mr. Joe Gross goes from the second floor to room 2301 in his building. . . . The new address of the Rolf family of Dubuque will be 7815 Glenn Plaid Avenue, Inglenook, California. . . ." The third hour of the address was devoted to world addresses while the last half-hour was time for universal truths. The adults of America hung on until time for the Eleven O'Clock News. Then a cloud of depression would settle like heavy fallout over the streets and the cornways; the police with their dogs would be set on critical alert. After a light snack, a little sleep, there were few incidents.

Up five hundred feet, the clean winds could go free, but below they had to scramble through the alleys of the city. The city was furiously hot, fire boiling down under the streets in the sewers and the underground. The furnaces and ovens, stacked one upon another, rose up in a thermal upsidedown cake, an asbestos glove to slap down your orange juice. Peppery specks clashed in millions of pink honeycombed lungs. In November, 1963, over 400 New Yorkers fell down with "speck attack" raging in their chests.

Billy was relieved when Lois took his penis in her hand and told him that it was the biggest she had ever imagined. Lois wanted to kiss him there, but he was too nervous and instead they skipped through the preynini bushes to the oasis, where they could bathe in pineapple oil and sweet Vermont water. "What I wouldn't give for a nice sauna now," yelped Lois, her head full of shampoo.

"You bet," said Billy. He was examining some mysterious tracks in the mud out back of the wash shack. It seemed a bit larger than the human foot and with splayed toe-like limbs running in five or six directions.

Social science is like the science of human nature, at least that's the way Hobbes liked to think of it. He was the "father" of social science. Locke popularized Sensationalism. This was quite difficult for the older citizens of Europe to comprehend. It took Hartly to really explain it. But then Helvetius came along with his great faith in legislative reform and his belief that "self-interest" is always human nature. That was quite enough. Billy closed the book and went out to look for Lois at the hospital when the wire swung through his inner ear. He turned to see his attacker. Which direction first? Which attacker?

Man is the dirtiest animal. His pollution is driving him to look for an edge of the world which he can fall off. Yet he loves like no other animal. His beauty makes trees look like kings and his social science is able to explain almost any motivation. And his love and beauty, in a sense, are a pollution to the world. They spray emotion into green vegetation. Love is beautiful in the middle of the forest, and beside the bird sanctuary the gnarled hand scrawls out the right line. Every line is just there in Nature.

Billy was dried and in his clean, pressed white suit. Lex, his "boy," came softly like a gerbil to the foot of his tent pavilion. "Lex, get me a bottle of that champagne. The pink kind." The boy was off in a spray of dust. Billy sat down and opened his diary.

> Today I made it with the nurse, Lois. It was good and I thought it would never happen! She fell for the religious bit like a real sucker. Which, by the way, she is. She's from Rye, New York. One of those fools who thinks all Midwesterners eat nothing but jello salad. Anyway, tonight I'm giving her the works: champagne, kneaded pâté of giraffe, lion steaks, mousse of lippi grass, and afterwards a dose of TxuTxu's "medicine." Perhaps I'll invite the Chief.

Lois arrived wearing her lemon-colored cocktail dress and rope sandals. Lex served them slowly, graciously in the candle light. Billy was a warm, engaging host. He treated her to countless anecdotes and toasted her beauty five or six times.

The Dean moved to his window and turned back one of the drapes so that he could look out over the south campus. Hall thought the back of his head looked like a shriveled-up and hairy gray buttock. That made him think of a cute ass he had seen in his eleven o'clock.

"Mr. Hall," the Dean spoke without turning from the window, with his left arm hooked behind his back in military pompous affectation. "You don't even understand what Time is, do you?"

"Minutes, hours, that sort of thing?"

"Mr. Hall, do you know what the rate of change is doing to the people of this earth? To the advanced people, the cutting edge of humanity. It's playing them at the wrong speed, like Frank Sinatra coming through your head at 78 so he sounds like Donald Duck and the Chipmunks, and all you can do is keep moving, moving. Where do you think you will move to after I expel you, Mr. Hall?"

Right to your bullshitting throat!

"Arhh, I thought I would get a job and then try and get a commission in the Coast Guard. That was Dad's outfit, sir."

"Bach will sit over here and across from him will be Mr. Handel. And then Mozart at this end, put Lorry next to Mozart, will you, Don."

Nikolaus sat patiently for all four hours of the meeting. He had heard these debates weekly for the last two years at Lettey University. The Left was always in trouble, the Administration was always winning, it was always the same story. You couldn't get the neutrals to take the demonstrations seriously. The fraternity jocks wouldn't bother you until you had a demonstration, and then they went berserk and clobbered you. So it was the same old story. Then Marsha came up and walked out of the hall beside him into the brisk Minnesota night. It was so dark

| 73 |

with only the campus gaslights burning along Bicycle Path and Grayson Lake. Marsha was very short and bouncy. She was wearing no bra so her firm, high breasts tossed playfully under her thin blouse. Her hair was brown and soft and her face reminded one of a pixie.

"Let's take a walk, Nikolaus. How about it?" she said and took his arm.

"Sure," and they started off toward the University Golf Course.

They walked for twenty minutes or so and talked little. Just pointed at a favorite landmark or glanced at the sparkling crisp sky of the new winter here in the great middle of America, the backbone.

It was completely natural the way suddenly Nikolaus bent down and kissed Marsha, first softly and then sliding his tongue into her sweet mouth, which was wet for him and slightly sour and good. They stood there beside the Twelve Hole for about ten minutes, hugging harder and kissing deeper. Then, gently Marsha kneeled down in front of him and he went to kneel too, but she motioned to him that he should stand, and then she gently and innocently kissed him lightly on the penis through the rough fabric of his jeans. Then she pulled him down into her arms and they rolled over and over, rolled down onto the slight knoll at the edge of the smaller sand traps.

Marsha's panties were down around her calves in the wet grass, and she was chilly as a globe of her pink ass slipped out from under the pleated skirt of Royal Stewart plaid she had bought in Atlanta two years before. Nikolaus was mouthing her vagina, stroking his tongue in long sweeps up between the hot open lips and then driving it into the tight sphincter full of acrid juice. She was crying out very loud.

Then it was the other way around as she knelt over him and undid his zipper, then pulled, yanked his pants down, and saw his large erection like a bright pole come into the starlight. She nipped at it with her lips. Then circled the head of it with a slow, wet tongue. Then went down and took one of his testicles into her wet mouth and sucked gently so that he felt his very sexuality grow confused tugging in many directions. Then she tried to swallow his prick. But instead sucked it up and down in long delicate flows of energy and sensation.

He turned her on her back and took his time easing into her slippery warm belly. Then he would rotate and swivel, drive, lunge, and stroke until he suddenly stopped and she would keep going . . . whimpering and bucking and sucking his pole and then he would go again. He balled her. He made love like that for an hour and then finally he came deep into her. They were both full of exhaustion.

"That had absolutely no redeeming artistic value. I was simply fucking," said Nikolaus.

Later, his hands under his head and looking at the ceiling from his dark bed in the dorm, Nikolaus thought how odd it was that now that he could have all the sex he wanted, the world was becoming more and more messy. The sexual revolution was a strange thing, he thought.

Perhaps it wasn't a good revolution. But what the fuck is a good revolution? A good fuck, probably. Anyway, he had class at nine.

Billy was reading from his *History of Western Culture* while Lex prepared Lois for the ceremony. Her hands are tied behind and above her head, her bust thrown out and her ankles tightly bound. Lex cranks her up to the ceiling with Billy's winch attachment—we take you now into the book: Jesus was the most crucial man insofar as he was of the species, more important perhaps than Adam, for he was both the Gift of God. . . . Billy put the book down and took a sip of his pink bubbly. "My God, Lois, you certainly look ravishing up there!"

She shook her head but was tightly gagged with a British flag-scarf. Billy finished his wine and swung his legs off the couch. He took up the whip gently, testing it slowly, teasingly running its scaly tip through his fingers. It was fifteen feet long and as red as fire. "This is going to hurt you, Lois. Let me assure you."

> Was the beginning of the bomb
> The end of the line?
> Don't ask the linear men
> And a bottle of rum.

"Gordon, this honky claims to be one of us." They were standing in the secret warehouse, the new headquarters of the Detroit Epileptic Movement.

"What is your name?"

"Billy, sir," he said. He was wearing a black silk jacket embroidered in gold, blue, and red with a glaring tiger and underneath the words "Khe Sanh."

"What's your last name, Billy?" Gordon was very calm and leisurely at the onset of an interrogation.

"Billy Fencer, sir."

"Where you get that jacket, Billy?"

"I got it in a poker game in West Lhoopville."

"The geese are running hot tonight."

"No soap, radio."

"Well, I guess you really are one of us. You know the new code riff and all that. With the Helping Hand, I presume?"

"That's it. I'm a courier right now. Got a message for you."

"What I want with a message? Me, I'm happy with no messages, like no message is the best message, that's my media, you dig?"

"From Thaddeus Mace," said Billy, standing just a little taller as he heard his own words bounce off the far walls of the flashlight warehouse.

"All right then, shoot," said Gordon. But one of his lieutenants, one Immanuel, misunderstood and fired fifteen big slugs out of his scatter gun. The black souvenir jacket was suddenly a delta full of blood rivers. Billy was sobbing through his death pain. Gordon couldn't believe the dumb mistake and slapped his forehead, then pulled an orange dart off his belt and jabbed it into this Immanuel's chest. A super nausea dart always fatal after two days of paralysis and seizure.

"Weep not for me, weep . . . weep for . . . America because . . . weep for her . . . because," Billy was trying to remember the coded message. Gordon was on his knees, his ear pressed to dying lips. After a few seconds, the people in the cold warehouse saw a wave of vibrations pass down the thin body, and then Gordon rose up.

"What was that he talk?" asked Debby.

"We're going to move Heaven and Earth. We are going to run across streets and play on three sides of every track. We are going to taste the emptiness that comes in the world's biggest ice cream cone. Right at the very bottom." Gordon finished his speech and walked quickly to his blown V-8.

THE CONFERENCE MAN

The Conference was scheduled to last three days in February. Bob Day arrived at the City Airport near dinner time and quickly contacted Miss Ringle.

"We have booked a room for you at the Old Amsterdam. Is this your first trip in Drear City?"

"I believe it is," answered the tall detective.

"Then stay under wraps. We'll get you a cover by noon tomorrow. I'm looking forward to meeting you. Perhaps on the floor around seven?"

"That would be fine," he said.

The taxi driver looked suspicious. Day checked him out with the medicine routine he learned long ago. The man passed. The Old Amsterdam was one of those hotels where film grips used to lose their fruitcakes in Her Majesty's time. Bob Day went to the bar for a drink before checking in. There seemed to be one gun there, possibly two. Also a cute number. Nothing hard to bring down. He toasted himself and went to annoy the desk clerk. Day always annoyed these guys. If you travel over two hundred thousand miles a year, you learned to string together time with a series of rituals, chiefly insult and cruelty, an occasional sex experience. Like unwrapping the cellophane from the bathroom waterglass. You had to look into the theatrical mirror and smile. A thin ridge of shiv around the mouth. Eyes two bits. Two bits a shave. A haircut and a fruitcake, a movie and then bed.

The next morning dawned early. Bob Day was up and covering his special shoes in waterproof. An old service ritual. He unwrapped another glass and poured himself a slug of whiskey from the bottle that was always in his briefcase. Then called down for juice, eggs, plenty of toast, and extra butter. He liked sausage, but only in New England. This Conference was bound to be something just a little bit tough. The way Bob Day liked it. He moved around his room like a moveable cage. Inside his brain, the silver mask was waiting.

"Have you cleared this with Style?"
"Listen, Miss Ringle, listen I'm doing only my job and what I thought you wanted. Now Mr. Downs told me this was supposed to be released by eight-thirty. If you want

me to take it to Style then I will. But it won't be ready for the eight-thirty." Sylvester had a hard time with this woman. She and her channels. Sylvester was on his first expense account trip and he was in danger of blowing it because of Style. He hated Style Department and Pearl Gulder. Suddenly an icy finger jabbed the soft spot under his ear and he grunted astonishment. He turned to see a tall blond man wearing a silver mask, frowning.

"Take this to Style. Do as Miss Ringle tells you. Now go. . . ." He wasted no time.

"Thanks, Bob."

"Nothing. Now listen, Clara, I want to ask you a question. On this job I get all the benefits?"

"Don't be euphemistic, Bob. What do you mean?"

"I want you, Clara, and you know that. I'm tired of being your lover and never loving you. Always going off behind closed doors with the big execs and their filthy parties, the corporate garbage circuit. This is what I work. Sometimes I lay awake at night and look at the ceiling and think, maybe socialism would be better, even socialism. I want a wife and two kids and a home to drive home to. I want to have time to kick it around."

Clara Ringle took his arm in her soft hand and pressed herself quickly to his side and then released him, but her presence was still on him. She liked this man more than words could ever say. They had met at a small meeting when both of them were young and had uncertain futures. They had been young and in each other's hair, in each other's futures and in each other's beds and in each other's houses for dinner in the dawn of young adulthood. Clara was determined to become a leading figure in the Industry. Day was a lone wolf. The two of them moved through their paces with the grace of an insider and an outsider, like two sprouts twirling around a pole, into embrace. Into the embrace, she loved this man. She respected.

"I want to take you home with me, Bob. Tonight, later, forever."

"That's not enough. Do I get all the benefits this time, not just the substance, the lemon meringue filling? I want a promise out of you, Clara."

She heard the frontier stretch her moans. She had so little time before the first seminar, and still she wanted to possess.

"You'd better go now, Bob. I will see you later. On the floor. Take care. I care so much. I really do." She briskly turned and walked back into the temporary press headquarters. A tear had been promised but never delivered.

The lone wolf in the world of ice.

The perfectability of man. In his quietism, he could see the frozen north or the frozen south, the white east or the white west. He was lost in the perfectability. That is, he was lost. The progress he had been making had made itself into a receding line placed directly on top of its identical. Bob vowed that he would never let himself go hungry, go wild if he lived through this.

"Excuse me, could I see your room? I work for Joseph Josephson Brothers. I am afraid this is compulsory." The short fat man had his tie in his hand. He had been preparing for dinner when Bob Day came to search his room. The man's name was Hirky. He didn't like this. Day was some kind of private investigator. He had nothing to hide from him, but this was a breach of privacy, an incredible intrusion. He stayed put.

"What?"

"Look, mister. I don't enjoy this, this is my job. I know you heard what I said, I spoke loud and clear. I would appreciate your just letting me in, and I'll take as little of your time as possible."

"Are you kidding? I want to see some kind of identification. Who are you?" Hirky was sweating.

Day looked down slowly at his right hand where it just hung, half-clenched, by his gray flannel trousers. There was a blurting metal. Hirky traced his eyes down to the hand, saw the flash, tried quickly to forget it, could hear his heart jump-jumping to his nose. He stepped back a defeated figure.

"Thanks," said Day. He stepped inside. The room was identical to his own. The best place would be the curtain hems. These were clean. Then the Swiss lamp, but this too was clean. He went quickly through the suitcases and the dirty linen bag. No. He shook hands with Hirky and apologized. "This is a rotten job," he told him.

"No kidding," said the man.

After this, he would find out exactly what he was supposed to be looking for from the boys in Josephson Brothers. The big execs, the living and breathing garbage. He hated their guts. The hotel corridor was very long, and Day decided to walk down to the end and see what the view from the window, from the rear of the hotel, was like and also to give himself a chance to unwind. That Hirky had been a decent man. He would have reacted the same way. He would have noticed the metal sooner, though. That was his job.

"Clara, who is this Mr. Robert Day?"

"He's a special investigator we have used for years. He knows how to work conferences better than anyone else in the world. He's a legend. I'm surprised you never heard of him."

"I always left Security to the Staff, you know. Now what are we going to do with the Miller proposal? I don't see how we can cut back the office budget and still be able to turn out two biennials, plus the Puerto Rican brochure. Also, Willy Hornsby is hot for a new amendment in the constitution that would allow him to take more money directly over Arthur's signature. They want to double production in two years. I don't blame him, but I hardly see how it's possible." Mr. Kristin was Mr. Josephson's representative. Over the years, he and Clara Ringle had come to an understanding that allowed them to go on talking and go on thinking simultaneously. After exchanging views, they would pick each other's brains, read each other's thoughts, run it down, run it up. Clara could keep up with any man. That is the reason, men thought, the reason she doesn't need me. They never knew how one part of her brain was set aside. Was frozen soul. Only Day had ever trodden in such white territory, and then it had been when both were young. He had been a voyager in the heat of her soft, little rose, her easy rider, he had launched a moment of peace in her. She poured half a cup of coffee and tried to read the figures Kristin was underlining on the board. She sat down. She wondered where that poor man was.

The Grand Ballroom began to fill at about seven-thirty. There were seats for five hundred delegates, twenty trustees, thirty-five ushers, one detective. The press was barred.

Day sat in the darkened corner of the Tom Paine Hearth-room. All around him was the din of delegates. He had a glass of beer in his hand, a frown on his face. The delegates were proving an unwieldy mass. He had found one spy and one impostor. Still, there was something else at the heart of the matter. Something not right at the heart, but right near the heart. Something ready to pounce on the heart and puncture its action. He had no sure knowledge. He was a detective without a real mandate. And he had done what he was being paid for: weeded out the attitudes. This was not a bad bunch of men. They had their work and their lives and their three daughters apiece and their red cars built low to the ground with a hot scar in their tails. But there was something slanted, close to the center, threatening the movement, worrying Day. He shook his head. He shook it off. It would not leave.

The Grand Ballroom was almost full when he took his seat. Hot under the yellow arc lights, eyes scorched after the cool darkness of the bar, he tugged at something on his face. A piece of skin. It wouldn't come off. The man in front of him was asleep. His wife was reading a small calorie counter and tugging at the fur around her shoulders. Across the aisle there was a group of young men from red-faced country. They had their shirts off. No . . . that hadn't happened. They had on pink shirts and white ties and had their jackets off. He shut his eyes and felt the air hover in his silver mask box. He was wandering down a dark hall until the electric bell went clang, and the meeting was called to order. They were such waiters, that is, they patiently sat. He looked off at the wall. They were looking for a sure thing. Every one of them looking for the sure thing. He looked at the lady with the brown fur piece and the calorie counter. Her face was reminiscent of a pile of gears softly rounded into one another and covered with dreadful calm. The high black eyelashes and the thin ridge of nose, whose tip was a beautiful blubber, an orange pop over the blur of her lips. He wondered what her secret was and if it were expensive. He wanted out. The meeting had scarcely just come to order and he was tired to death. Now he contended with the death of a crowd.

Up on the dais, Clara was scanning the crowd for a sight of Bob Day. It was hopeless. She had her notes in her hand and was not concerned about the speech she would soon be making. The arc lights made her skin dry, she felt. She had on a tan wool suit and a tan leather purse. Day was around somewhere. He usually sat in row one. She couldn't see him. She thought about the difference between Day and Mr. Josephson. Why should one be the rich man and the other the legendary underling?

Because of inheritance? It did not seem fair. This was America of the Sixties. She straightened a stocking and remembered that eyes must surely be on her now. A warm smile. Perhaps his eyes?

The crowd was on fire. Bob Day moved to the left apron near the foot of the dais. If they wanted to go for Josephson, he would get to him first. If they wanted to ignore Josephson, maybe he would get him all by himself. No, he forgot, he was Josephson's man. He moved in his silver container flight, his hand perspiring a blue storm. His tight rig in its trigger. *Got hold on to mind.* He felt for his composure up there. Under arc lights. They were really screaming. His badge turned upside-down. Were there any city dicks in the place? The security goons were extra dumb tonight. One thin redhaired man with gorilla lips was carried to the door by that Italian goon. He must have got his training in the Coco Pareda thatched hut patrol. His finger cocked and trigger. His wild horse right on the beam. There she was up there, the nerve, the right reason of it.

The riot lasted for twenty minutes. It began with a dirty word and ended with a silver bullet. The stranger got away up the back steps, but not before a young lady got a lock of his hair. Day had known something was wrong near the heart. It turned out to be the reds and the redhaired man especially. They had to get him to the office. If they could, maybe this thing could be prevented from ever repeating itself. At least in his lifetime. He was bound to hear from her, he knew that. He could not blame her either. Things had gotten pretty hot in that hall. He had never seen anything like it in business circles. He lay down on his mussed bed and kicked his brown loafers off. He stared at his toes. The socks were soaked completely through. The phone rang.

"Bob Day?"

"Speaking." He was staring at his toe.

"This is Lynn Williams. From the Bureau."

"Go ahead. I'm listening."

"We want to know if you have any idea who started this thing in the Ballroom tonight."

"You guys don't mess around."

"The Toad was there. One of our men saw him."

"Sorry. I checked that myself. It was a guy, believe it or not, the spitting image of the Toad. Not him. Not at all." It pleased him to tell the Bureau this. They were such competent men. They had wanted him to join up for years. Ever since the Dong Ho assassination.

"Listen, Bob. Did you know the Josephson Brothers?"

"Never been in the same room with them before tonight."

"Then you didn't know they were dealing drugs down the Canadian Bosom, you know, straight to Buffalo and after that the nation. Did you?"

"I don't believe it."

Day moved slowly about his room. Lacing up a pair of boots. Dialing a dead telephone. Waiting for some kind of contact. He had a bottle sent up and some hot food.

He took off his clothes and sat naked in the dark, staring at the Buck River. He got a chill and took a hot shower. His temperature hit a hundred and two. His trigger finger was slowly curling into a baby's knuckle, a barnacle of rust.

Clara, on the St. Lawrence Seaway, tugged at her fur piece and went out on deck. She wondered if Day would stay holed up in that room forever. The stupid fool. She had once needed him. For one moment.

The Josephson Brothers fell in the foyer of a hotel in Winnipeg. The Mounties drew and retained their massive power on the wings of a terrible beating. The five of them. Barry Josephson went down first. Meg, his secretary, fell dead over a lamp in a moment of horror. Finally Joseph Josephson was shot down as he fled through the kitchen. A poor old man who had been hiding underneath one of the giant chrome stoves came out and stood over the petrified body. He spat on it and said disgustedly, "*Cochon?* American gangbuster!" The Mountie pushed him aside. Only Clara escaped. She took a taxi directly to the station. She knew now what had happened and how she must get to him. How could he ever understand?

The phone continued to ring.

Target practice at the screen of the television, going click instead of pulling the trigger. He was completely naked on the crumbs of his rumpled cot. The pipes were chattering like Boston Harbor. He was weak and almost dead now. No wonder.

The phone rang. He ignored it. It rang again moments later. He answered.

"Day, it's me."

"Hello!" He felt particularly soaked.

"This is Clara Ringle. I have got to come up there. I have got to explain it all."

"I see here the Brothers were brought down up North."

"Oh, Day!"

"You shake out of your mind and you leave me sitting. I was a simple man. But no more. I wanted you over and off the wall. The thing is, I feel like my heart is . . . broken is the word you don't come. . . ." He had never known sobs. So soft and thick. Too bad he had come so late to their swells on this cotton bench. He covered the mouthpiece and she lit a frantic cigarette in her booth. It was raining in Christmas City. He coughed and spoke to her:

"If you ever come up here, I'll use your head for a bat. I swear I will do you into a mush-head. I will. Now shove. . . ." He slammed it down.

The wings of her surprise flung straight against the sinew, the fever coming down in the rain. She had never doubted that he would have her. She walked toward Avenue C. The black tar with a hideous spectre and the dim grocerías tucked into the walls. Her yellow raincoat was too fresh for this neighborhood. The cigarette smoked down to her finger.

Bob Day sat still. On his cot. He sobbed. He watched football, hockey, and movies. He ate beans and steak, drank whiskey, and smoked his brand. He took his time and he waited without any reason to wait.

One day he was better. He rose from the hotel and took a taxi to the airport. He had cashed another check. A coin for the man at the shoeshine parlor, the same man as before.

"What you been up to, Mr. Day? Long time, no see!"

"Murray, can you get me a meeting with the Bureau?"

"Two minutes," said the man and put his rags down. He walked inside his little stall and picked up a phone, dialed, and spoke. Two minutes later he put the receiver down. "Chicago, Wrigley Field, the tenth at 1:00 P.M."

Day gave him a handful of silver.

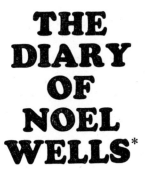

THE
DIARY
OF
NOEL
WELLS*

Depressed, depressed, depressed. I've been down in the dumps ever since Philip left for Africa. The life around here is really stagnant. Philip arranged for me to have my own car and driver on call at all times so I wouldn't have

* Noel Wells wrote this section of her diary while living as a guest in the mansion of fabulous capitalist Thaddeus Mace, whose son Philip she had recently agreed to marry. The Mace estate is the largest private estate in the Bahamas. Thaddeus Mace, and recently his son Philip, have in addition to their great financial holdings long been noted for their selfless service in behalf of the United States Government.

to deal with the Whale, which is what I call his mother. She is really too much. She is a member of about fifteen million clubs and spends all her time talking to various club members on the phone. These are clubs in New York and San Francisco and Washington and long-distance calls.

Philip wouldn't tell me exactly what kind of oil deal he was going to make in Africa, in fact he didn't even mention oil but I imagine that is what the deal is about because before he left his father kept briefing him on all these different men who operated in the oil "game" as Mr. Mace calls it. He was going to the Congo and on his way back he says he will probably have to stop in both Miami and La Paz, Bolivia. He said he might not be back for six weeks.

Have I explained to you about Philip's guns? He wears these two pistols in holsters under his suit jacket. They are very dark blue and in the sun they are enormously impressive. He wears them because he is very rich and says that many people are jealous of his position and might try and take revenge on him for being richer than they are. I guess that's a pretty good reason. I know that I feel safer being with him because he has the guns. I asked him if he had ever killed anybody and he said he had killed seven men. I asked him who and he said that they had all been maniacs out to hurt either him or his father. I guess life as a Mace will be very exciting if not always typical.

I don't do much of anything. I am starting to write poetry after having talked so much about it with Manda. I showed her this poem I wrote about a scene I saw when Chris and I visited Guatemala last month. It was pretty short:

> The horses run rakes in long fields
> Of night here in Guatemala, the girls
> Dance on the seeds hoping for yields
> And after dark the boys caress their curls
>
> Peasant father and peasant mother
> How glad to finish the days trip
> Their faces are like voyages to another
> Time to healthy appetite and tight grip
>
> Lizards creep out of the barns
> The ox is off in heavenly sleep
> While grandma the socks darns
> And the dog brings home the sheep.

I guess it isn't exactly great but Manda seemed to really like it. The title is "Lizards Creep Out." Philip thinks it is really silly writing poetry because nobody buys it any more. He said that if I wanted to write he could get me a job writing the news scripts for the local Nassau television station which is part of Mace Communications. There is one guy here, his name is Wally Norton, and he is the main news broadcaster. In fact, he is the second best in the country after Durlon Dean who is the stateside commentator at seven o'clock. They keep Wally Norton here because he is Thaddeus Mace's favorite broadcaster and the only television show that he will watch is Wally Norton's Scoop On the World which is on at six-thirty here.

I've begun to worry about what ever became of Alex

Washer, the boy who I went with all through Jefferson. Alex had the blondest hair I've ever seen on a boy and big blue eyes and a tiny perked up nose that was adorable. He had a blue T-bird that was blown and stroked and with tons of chrome. I mean, it was all so high school. But you know I get these nostalgia rushes. I just lay down for hours and start to go back over things that happened years ago and it's really beautiful, like actually living your youth over again. I mean, at least we can never have them take our memories away from us even if we have to get old and lose the freedom of high school.

Alex was the first boy I ever slept with. He was also the second boy I ever kissed with tongue and mouth open. We really grew up a lot together, educated each other. I was remembering the Prom, the Junior, the other night and how it had been with Doris Taylor and her date Paul Imperiales and me and Alex all at the same table. The theme was "Wild West" and the gym looked just like that show Comanche Trail that is now off the air I think. Paul and Doris brought this bottle of gin in Doris's raincoat. That was strictly not allowed. We would have been expelled from Jefferson if they had caught us with that. Now, it's really funny how you get when you're in your twenties, I'm already twenty-four, it's like a dream. But it just occurred to me how stupid we had been to have taken those chances just for a little thrill. I didn't even like to drink and I don't think Alex really did or the others. But I mean we just had to be so impressive and big for the others, you know. It's funny, the teachers were right not to trust us. We were irresponsible kids.

That night I made the Court, as one of the Prom Queen's torch guardians, and I was really happy even though I expected to. I knew I would make at least that but not the Queen itself. I was not that popular and Cathy Flinch was sure to take it. From what I understand, that night she really took it because her date got sick and puked all over her dress which had cost something like a hundred and fifty dollars in Boston. She deserved it actually, her and her Cape Cod "cocktail parties" all summer, to hear her tell it.

Alex, Alex, I wonder where you are tonight. Out there in the darkness of this night. My memories take control of me for a moment and I imagine once more being back with you in the car out on the Bluff. I miss you and wonder where you are.

The Whale just came through and said that Mr. Mace had told her that he might have some word from Philip tonight at dinner. I hope so. I guess I can bear another silent dinner here even though lately I've begun taking them downtown or out at Cole's Island with Manda or some of the other people out there.

Alex once took me to this motel in Connecticut for two nights and all we did was make love and I peeled these green grapes, huge juicies, and then put them in my mouth and kissed him and transferred the grape into his mouth by squirting. He thought it was really erotic! I loved to do that. Maybe when Philip gets back I'll do that with him.

Mr. Mace has heard from Philip and said that all was well in the Congo and that he might be able to stop back over here for a quick visit before going on to Bolivia in three weeks or so.

Today I got up early and ran downstairs and it was a beautiful day so I called up this girl named Melanie Warburton and asked her if she wanted to go sailing and we agreed to meet at the club in an hour. So we got there and the first five minutes out of the dock a storm came up and we sat on the island for the entire day. I had to spend the rest of the day and night reading.

Manda and I had lunch at Pinocchio's and then went to the little "scotch" beach. We were sunning and talking about art and also rock music when these two men appeared out of nowhere. One was Swedish and the other was from Finland. The Swedish man was not what you would expect. He had dark hair and skin and was sort of hairy and chunky, not at all a Viking type. But he explained that he was part of the Swedish people descended from invasion of Serbian or Slovakian or something! type of people. He was very nice though and his name was Rudy. We talked, the four of us, for a long time about the island's particular style of living and the foreigners' impressions of it. Then, Manda and the Finnish man, who was very tan and tall, went for a long swim.

Rudy and I lay there on the beach and watched them. And we kept talking about things like his country and New York and topless bathing suits. And then we entered into this sort of uptight phase, a thing in which you sort of run out of words and just lay there and stare at your toes. This phase, in my experience, usually means you're both thinking about S—E—X, invariably. I knew that I would have to tell Rudy when the time came if it did, that I was engaged and not interested in any little extracurricular fun and games. I was thinking this when suddenly Rudy just as naturally, as matter of factly, as if there was nothing at all out of the ordinary in his actions, reached with his left hand right on my crotch. And he squeezed really gently and said, "This feels good and soft, I like to touch you there. You don't mind?" and then he kissed me and I was really surprised to find that I liked it. Anyway, he got his hand all the way into my pants and was really going at it and I kept thinking, Why don't you stop him? Yet I knew I really didn't want to. I mean, I sort of did not like it and found it very scary but more of me seemed to just melt under his fingers and I almost passed out there. My head went back on the spread and I had this image of his dark fingers going in and out of my hole and felt them curl down and then up into the muscle of my womb. Oh, Philip, I probably could never explain to you how I felt, how confused I was.

Fortunately, Manda and the Finnish man came back from their swim afterwards. He had tried to pull my pants off altogether but at this point I absolutely refused. My God, I was so embarrassed. Manda acted as if she knew nothing at all but I was sure she knew exactly what had been going on. After all, the beach in that hot sun is not exactly a place to hide something, I mean a normal lover's lane or anything. Rudy acted quite relaxed as if nothing had happened and I am afraid I must have been blushing something awful. Well, we stayed and talked about little things for another hour though my heart wasn't in it at all. I was terribly confused about what had happened. I mean, Philip so far away in such an unpleasant place as Africa and me his fiancée not even able to be faithful to him for a whole month. I kept thinking that maybe Chris had been right when he once called me a "mature baby" and said that I had a lot of growing to do yet even if I already knew a lot of things. To allow Rudy to paw me out in public like that had been absolutely immature. Thank God when Manda said she had to get to her painting lesson so we could leave the beach and part with these Nordic men. As I left Rudy I gave him a friendly goodbye though I must say not a very enthusiastic one and he grabbed my arm and held it. I tried to pull away but he wouldn't let go and Manda and Lars were up ahead already saying goodbye so they didn't see how rude he was. He said, "You'll see me again won't you." It wasn't even a question!

I told him to please let go of my arm and that I regretted very much what had happened on the beach because I was engaged already to someone else and very much in love. I asked him to respect my reputation and try not and brag about what he had gotten down on the beach from me. He still had a hold on my right forearm. So I tried to rip my arm free and then he let go and he laughed and said, "Being engaged is nothing. I'll see you soon." And then he winked and tried to kiss my cheek. I almost broke into tears because I had no effect on him, he was determined to try and see me again.

When I asked Manda if she had seen what had happened on the beach between Rudy and myself she said of course, and she said, "You're lucky. He's quite a hulk isn't he." I was shocked by her total amorality as she knew I was engaged to Philip. But then I realized that she played around so much that she probably expected everybody else to be just like her. Manda is getting old, at least she has to put on a lot of make-up and liner and I feel she is just as hostile to me as she is friendly because of my younger complexion. At first I thought she was really exciting but now I find I cannot respect her. At least, not as much as at first.

When I got home I felt so bad I slept through dinner and then Ramon, one of the Mace servants, came up with a nice tray of fruit compote and sherbet. After I ate this I went back to sleep. The next day I got up early and decided to take a hike out on the Mace ranchero, which is what they call this peninsula of the island that they own and which is used half as a vegetable farm and half as a radar tracking station and a small base of soldiers which is mostly underground. It is a great place for a hike since they have marked out special hiking trails for the Mace guests to follow and every mile there is a little pavilion rest area with a water fountain and picnic table. Also the trees are labeled like in botanical gardens and sometimes ponds have little markers that tell you what the various kinds of birds around the water are and the water bugs and the lilies. I set out with Carol, a secretary to the Mace family and a friendly companion. Mrs. Mace never lets me do anything alone. If I'm not going to be with friends she makes sure one of the secretaries goes with me. This can be a big pain but I was glad on that day because I really didn't feel like being alone. The thing with Rudy had gotten to me.

In any case, we hiked and then had a picnic down by a completely deserted beach which was lovely. You would have never known that there was civilization nearby except that this Army helicopter kept hovering around at all times. They keep the peninsula very well guarded. Carol started talking about this yacht trip she had taken all over the Bahamas a few summers before and it was very interesting because she had been with this Venezuelan businessman and his party and they had thrown the wealthiest parties she had ever been to. She had had an affair with one of this businessman's sons, a boy named Enrique. He had been sort of crazy and kept talking of philosophy of science and something else which I forget which completely impressed Carol. She kept saying, "He knew all about the philosophy of science. The philosophy of science." He had been a student at some college in New York State, a Catholic school. Anyway, Carol told me this long story of the trip including how Enrique got drunk and wanted to fight a duel with the captain of the boat who was named Captain Page but how the Captain had been forced to go chicken in fear of Enrique's father's money. And then this boy Enrique had claimed that the man had lost all his honor so he was now the captain of the ship. Then the captain got angry and was going to fight the duel and then Enrique's father got angry, he was very drunk, and pulled out his wallet and offered Page one hundred thousand dollars for his ship and Page had to accept because the ship was only worth about seventy thousand. And then when he had accepted the money the father punched him very hard and knocked him out and then they all went back below while somebody carried the captain to his cabin. After that, Enrique was in charge and he got them lost and they had to call the Coast Guard to come and tow them into Miami.

We got back from the hike around four and I took a nap.

I was walking into this dress shop downtown when I felt this tap on the back of my neck and I turned around and almost jumped a mile. It was Rudy. He was wearing these short shorts and blue sneakers and this red and white striped polo shirt which I thought was extremely loud. He kissed me on the cheek before I could duck and then asked me to come to lunch. It was three days since the "episode."

I should have slapped him. I guess I didn't because I felt so embarrassed at seeing him. I could still feel his rough fingers on my vagina.

I absolutely refused to have lunch with him. So then he insisted that I go for a drink with him. I told him absolutely N—O! Then he said he was not going to leave me until I accepted his offer. I said he had better or else I would call the police. He laughed. Anyway, I went into the shop to try and avoid him but he waited outside even after an hour of trying on dresses. Then I went to the Hotel Creole Victorian and tried to escape him by having a facial but there was a long line and then I tried calling a friend who had a suite in the hotel but she wasn't in. And then I tried walking down Mace Street but he wouldn't give up, all the while he was right at my side with this confidence that you wouldn't believe! So finally, I guess it was inevitable really, I had to give in and go for one drink in order to ditch him. He took me to this place called the Maserati Pit. It was this little bar in a wood building that was frequented by racing fans and owned by an ex-race car driver. He ordered me a banana daiquiri without even asking me and a Gin Rickey for himself. I asked him why he was so rude as to order me a drink without even asking me what my preference was. He said that banana daiquiris were his little aphrodisiac and I ought to at least allow him a fighting chance in his struggle with my virginity. I laughed and said that my "virginity" was not really very important any more but that my honor was and that I was engaged and that just by sitting in a bar alone with him I was disgracing myself and my fiancé. He was really conceited and paid absolutely no attention.

He had this way of smiling that was so goddamned self-confident I felt like kicking him.

Anyway, eventually I decided my best strategy was to keep absolutely quiet and pay no attention to him. But then he started talking about his childhood in Sweden and about how in the winters they had gone on these skiing trips all over Sweden, Norway, and Finland. He described these trips as very gay times with boys and girls sleeping together and switching partners every night and pranks like playing naked soccer in the snow on some hilltop north of the Arctic Circle. And then he started telling me about how he had once been engaged. She had been an orphan from Stockholm, he was from a small town in the middle of Sweden, and they had gone together for three years. And then she had died of cancer. It had been cancer of the liver, something really rare. He told me about his fiancée as if he was just telling any old story, almost as if he had a philosophy that when things went wrong you should try and bury your feelings in action, that feelings and action were not the same thing at all. So I asked him if weeping wasn't both a feeling and an action and he said that it was usually just a surrender to emotion and not a real action. So then I asked him what kind of action he had taken when his fiancée had died. He smiled very slightly but didn't say anything. I pressed him on it and he said that I would probably be shocked. I asked him why, if he had gone out and slept with another girl right away or what. Then he said that no, he had gone homosexual for two years. I'll say he shocked me! Not that I have anything against homosexuals at all but this Rudy certainly hadn't been acting like one with me down on the beach or then this afternoon. He said that he had fallen in love with another man and that for two years they had lived together and then one day he had decided that he wanted to end the affair. Then he had gone back to being a heterosexual. I asked him if he ever thought of going back to homosexual sex and he said no.

So this bit of surprise had the effect of opening me up

to a conversation with him. Before I had always thought of this man as part of the incident on the beach and suddenly I was listening to his most intimate secrets. It was funny because now that I think of it I realize what a good technique Rudy had in making me receptive to his seductions. By telling me intimate secrets he made me unconsciously start telling him some of my own inner thoughts. Like suddenly I was talking to him at that stupid bar about things that Philip and I had never discussed and probably never would because they just were not the kind of things we would ever discuss. For instance, I started in telling this stranger all about my thing with Chris from the very beginning up to the punch that he gave Philip. And I guess that was a real mistake. Rudy was a very good listener. Actually, he was enormously polite, the first real European man I had ever had anything to do with. It was strange. About forty minutes before I really hated him and suddenly here I was finding him a better conversationalist than the man I was going to marry. I really felt confused.

We talked a lot about my problems then after his confession. Rudy talked about Chris a little and thought that he sounded like an extremely selfish person. I realized that that was it. Chris was so selfish that he could only look on me as an object, he wanted nothing but "success." By success I mean he wanted to get in with the kind of people that I was now in with: Manda and the Maces. He just wanted me as a kind of plaything. That was why I had rejected him in the first place. I must have sensed that long ago but didn't finally realize it until Philip met me at the Thousand Faces reception in the spring. And then when he had asked me to be his guest down here, I understood how little my engagement to Chris meant. Chris was nothing like what I really needed. Rudy was right that afternoon when he said that it sounded like a life with Chris would have been very boring.

I had to leave but then ended up staying and talking to Rudy for about two hours longer than I had expected. So when I went to finally take a cab back to the Maces and he said that he wanted to see me again, I found it impossible to refuse. After all, I had led him on at this point and just couldn't cut him off so cruelly without explaining to him exactly why I felt it was wrong to even have just a talking relationship with another man. I agreed to meet him at this place, the Club Jailai, on Thursday night for a drink.

Carol and I spent the day out on Munson's Isle which is very close to this one. We had lunch at a fantastic luxury hotel there owned by the Maces and then went water skiing in this perfectly smooth lagoon. The water was so blue, it was unbelievably blue and clear and I told the man who took us skiing that I wanted to come back in a few days and try the skin diving there. He had recommended this to us.

The number of rich people there was absolutely amazing. When I say rich I mean really rich—oil millionaires and British people of the aristocracy with titles.

I had this dream about Chris last night that was really weird. I dreamed that I was in this room and wearing my Junior Prom dress which was all white and frilly. Then suddenly, I don't remember what exactly I had been doing but it was something like wringing out a washrag or a towel or something, I looked up from my seat at the window. Chris was standing in the window with his arms straight out at either side and his legs straight and together. It was like he was the crossed panes which separate windows into four smaller squares. I thought this was very interesting and I got up to look closer at him. Then he laughed at me and I asked him why. "Because I'm the window pane and that's symbolic like the pickle dish." Now I remember that the pickle dish was some kind of symbol I studied in high school somewhere in one of my classes. It's funny. Anyway, that was the end of my dream because I remember as I was waking up that I felt glad that he was the window because it might rain in on me and soak my new dress and he was protecting me.

Dreams are funny. I spent the day with Manda, but I didn't tell her about my date with Rudy. I've got to get ready for that now.

Sometimes it is even hard to write something because you are afraid that you will read it later and realize how stupid what you wrote was compared to what really happened. I'm not sure that makes much sense but it doesn't matter I suppose. I guess I should feel ashamed. But what good would that do? One part of me wants to confess everything to somebody here and then get out and go back to New York. Another part of me is perfectly content to repeat what happened all over again. And then another part of me just wishes Philip would hurry up and get home.

I saw Rudy this afternoon and he wants me to meet him at the club which Cole owns. I am not sure if I did the right thing but I said yes and planned on standing him up. Which is what I am going to do. He looked so goddamned smug and confident.

Yet, that's not fair either because he was so gentle and sensitive. In fact, I have never known a man who depended so much on how the woman felt not just on how he was feeling. I think European men are very very different from Americans.

Decided to go to the great lagoon on Munson's Isle again with Carol and do the skin diving which the man promised us was so great there. I did not meet Rudy at El Gitano so imagine that's that. And that is definitely for the best. Ramon drove us to the airport so we could take a helicopter to the island rather than the speed boat. I think Ramon is about the most handsome man on the island. He is very brown but it is a chocolate brown and not dark bittersweet-chocolate type. He says he is married and has five children which is amazing as he looks about twenty-five years old.

Skin diving was lovely. Except for all the water I kept swallowing. It is impossible to describe what it is like underwater in words. I mean, it is like entering another

world. There was one really frightening thing which was
this fish with a gigantic mouth which was all brown and
huge, HUGE! it must have weighed five hundred pounds.
This I found extremely frightening because I have never
been close to another living creature so much bigger than
myself unless it was at the zoo where the animals are kept
behind bars, naturally. Also especially interesting were
these fish colored a beautiful blue, royal blue. They kept
whizzing along the reef at steady paces as if they were on
rails or something. I think they are called parrot fish. I
was glad no sharks came around. Ha!

Later, on the beach, Carol and I had this argument
with a Spanish count about which was better athletically,
the U.S.A. or Europe. It was really hysterical because
neither Carol and I knew too much about any sports and
we had to defend stuff like American football, which is I
think soccer. He did admit though that Americans were
the best basketball players in the world but claimed that
this was because no other countries played basketball. I
knew this was absolutely untrue. They had the greatest
drinks at this café there, the bartender invents a new kind
of cooler or punch just about once a week. Carol told me
he was world-famous and had been featured in an advertisement in many magazines for some kind of whiskey. I
had not seen it.

Got back to the house and took a long hot bath and
then had a drink on the terrace. Mrs. Mace came up and
invited me to go to the casino with Mr. Mace and these
guests who own some kind of company that manufac-

tures liquid transistors or something. I agreed to go. This really surprised Mrs. Mace because I usually refuse these invitations. But tonight I felt in an especially cheerful mood. We had dinner which was very good—roast turtle, my first taste of that delicacy imported from the Yucatan. There is an island there which Mr. Mace owns, though it is unofficial. He keeps these giant pens of sea turtles there and a breeding station. It is one of the few islands, according to him, where sea turtles will lay their eggs.

After dinner Mr. Mace was feeling especially good so he decided to drive to the Casino in the horse carriage which is très elégant. He has these two big white coach horses to pull it and they are kept in a special barn out in back. They have a lot of saddle horses, used I guess for the annual hunt of the Nassau Hunt Club, but they are kept out on the peninsula where the radar station and the vegetable farm is.

The Casino was fun for about three minutes. I was given about two hundred dollars by Mrs. Mace to play with. She wanted me to play roulette but I hate that game because you lose so fast. So I played blackjack and found myself winning a little and then losing a little. It was like that all night. I think I ended up with about five or six dollars profit when I finally decided to quit. Mr. Mace and his guest, a Mr. Calliano, went to a private room for some kind of big money card game or something. Mrs. Mace lost some money at roulette and then went into the night club section to watch the show with Mrs. Calliano. I was really bored and should never have gone.

The next day I decided to write a letter to Mom. I haven't written to her in two months and am sure she wonders what has happened to her "little girl Noel."

Today I realized how gigantically bored I am. Have been ever since Philip left for the Congo. Oh, Philip, I wish you would hurry back. It's not fair to leave me like this during our "courtship" or whatever it is officially.

I think I am really mad at Philip. Went golfing with Carol and a guy named Mory Welt-Cottingham the Third. Get that. He is a fantastic golfer and a snob. Who wouldn't be with that name. At night we took motorbikes around the island; Carol, Mory, me, and a fellow named Randy Hoff.

Mrs. Mace says she is worried about me because I seemed bored. She told me she is going to tell Mr. Mace to tell Philip he had better return soon. Otherwise, she said, I may become so unhappy I'll start taking a "lover." I cringed when I thought of Rudy. Thank God that's done. I am a silly idiot and more immature than Chris realized.

I have been thinking about a funny idea which occurred to me. It's about making decisions. I mean I realized how important it is to make decisions and not delay them. This has always been my biggest problem because I just let things slide but never come to a conclusion about my real feelings. For example, with Chris I went with him for over a year even though I didn't really love him that much. I just refused to make the decision not to see him any more. It took Philip's invitation to his home to make me make a decision. Now that sounds complicated maybe, but I think it's a piece of real personal philosophy. It's the problem which has gotten me into the most trouble I think. Today I went skin diving again. I really like it underwater, it's so soothing because it's such another world. So silent.

Mrs. Mace thinks she may have to have an operation. She is flying to Boston to have tests.

At breakfast, I was reading the paper when Mr. Mace came in. He never has breakfast with me because he always is up by at least five-thirty in the morning to have his own breakfast, do laps in the pool, and begin work. I think he is a good friend of the President. I heard Ramon say that to one of his friends in Spanish the other day on the way downtown.

Anyway, he stopped and told me that he might have a surprise for me soon. I hope that means Philip.

Today it was overcast so I read and then went for a drive, then called a friend in New York. The Maces don't mind my making long-distance calls I found out. Finally I had to resort to watching television and went to bed early.

Carol and I went to a flamenco show downtown tonight. It was all right but the most interesting thing was this couple I saw. The girl was very tall and beautiful, she was Japanese. Her eyelashes were incredibly long and I don't think they were fake. The man was like a Viking god: tall, blonde, with a great build. He was wearing a white shirt, ordinary, and a pair of black leather jeans which were skin tight. She had on a dress that you could see right through, think she must have been wearing a body stocking.

Have been trying the new policy of making all my decisions right away and not putting them off. Like I told Manda immediately that I did not want to go to a party with her tonight whereas before I probably would have said, "I'll call you back later." Then ended up going even though I felt like going to this Spanish thing.

Mrs. Mace is in Boston.

Saw the couple, the Japanese and the Viking, out at Cole's Island. I don't know why they fascinate me so but they really do.

Mrs. Mace called and said that I was to use her appointment at the beauty parlor if I wanted it. I think I will because it is fantastic and I haven't been to one in years. Wait till Philip sees me with a new hair-do. I hope he'll like it—though I don't know if I'll even like it. Brenda Esterbank is having a party tonight.

Mrs. Mace arrived back today and said she was going to have the operation in the fall. It's some weird thing to do with her glands in her neck. I think it's her weight. It must be, she is such a whale.

Philip came back at noon! I am so HAPPY! He's going to be here for only two nights before going on to South America for a week and then home for good. But two nights is enough!

We took the cabin cruiser out alone for the night. It was so beautiful out there on the Caribbean. Philip is a fantastic captain. In the afternoon he showed me how to deep-sea fish but I didn't catch a thing. He caught two sharks. Yuk.

I can't tell you how romantic it is to be on your own yacht, with champagne on ice and steaks and a good sailor and a good lover. Because Philip is the greatest lover anyone could ever ask for. Anyone, anywhere. I know it.

In the morning we went swimming and then sailed back. It was really memorable—something words won't do any justice to. I am sad now though because in about ten minutes I'll have to go downstairs and drive Philip off to the airport. I wish he didn't have to go. I don't know if I can stand another miserable week alone after such a great two nights and the boat trip.

Today I did nothing but swim and read. I miss Philip. A lot. I am also mad at him. Very mad.

One thing I don't understand. Last night as we were driving to the airport he said something strange. He said, "By the way, the grabby guy is dead." I asked him what he meant. The second he said it I thought of Rudy because of the way he had grabbed me. I asked him what he meant but he wouldn't say anything else. Maybe he meant Chris. I don't know what he meant. I started wondering and I think I'm going to ask him when he gets back if he has killed anybody else since he told me he had killed seven men. That would be terrible, it would be murder if he had killed Rudy. He didn't deserve to die because of what he did to me. Though maybe he just died.

Carol and I went to a party at some new discotheque tonight and it was pretty bad. The food was good though. They had the best canapes I've ever seen and they tasted as good as they looked.

I got a letter from my mother. She had nothing to say. Just a bunch of news about a lot of people she thinks I remember but I don't. Oh, she enclosed some notice of engagement from a girl who was in my class: Cassie Evans. She is engaged to some guy from New Haven.

It was a beautiful day so I went to the beach with Manda. We met some interesting people from Mexico. The guys were awfully pushy though. As usual, Manda went off with one of them for a swim and I was left with this other eager playboy type. However, I used my new policy of making decisions right away.

This evening, I read and then watched television. I miss Philip a lot. Mr. Mace is in Washington.

MULTI

Instructions

You will need a blank piece of paper about the size of this page. Also a pen or pencil.

Draw a circle of approximately one inch diameter in the center of your paper. Fill it in. This is your Speck and the sheet is now your Speck Sheet.

Near the bottom of your Speck Sheet, write a multi-digit number, any number of digits you wish. This is now your Identification Number.

Now you must be screened. The process is quite simple. Merely press your Speck Sheet down against the Viewing Sheet (next page) for about one second. Make sure contact is firm and evenly distributed. Once this is done you will have been cleared and able to pass on through the Word Lock.

You may begin screening.

VIEWING SHEET

(approximate Speck position)

(approximate I.D. position)

Congratulations!

Now you have successfully completed your screening and are free to proceed through the Lock.

Your Speck is called   *Chris*

Reminder:

You will not be needing your Speck Sheet again until your next trip through the Word Lock when screening will again take place. Please be careful not to fold or mutilate your sheet.

This is Guide Voice. Your passage through the Word Lock was fine. At this time your particular Speck necessitates this taped data:

Welcome. This is Guide Voice. Your journey through the Word Lock was fine. At this time you will receive some historical data which you may already be familiar with. If this is the case, please bear with us.

The period we are concerned with is chiefly the second and third centuries of Planet-Village. Centuries in which P-V reconsolidation and efforts at outright apluralism were of prime importance, a period in which the most crucial indust-transpo techniques were jettisoned for the EFBS, the Experience Feeling Battery System.

Walter Westrum invented the Experience Battery in the year 179. With this piece of equipment a certain isolated experience could be contained within a zinc and lead battery, usually a D-cell battery in those pioneering days. Originally these batteries, the D-cells, were used for nothing but the most elemental electric charge. Once it was discovered that raw electricity could be "sculpted" through the ISO methods originated in the laboratory of Dr. Hauptman Bwemmerman, the invention of the Experience Battery was inevitable.

The Experience Battery revolutionized life on the P-V. Men became addicted to its use within a few decades. Indeed, it was so easily facilitated, one had simply to put the adhesive electrode from whatever battery one desired onto one's wrist or forehead and suddenly be swimming in the middle of the Mediterranean, eating a steak, making love, philosophizing, even sleeping—whatever individual experience was possible for man could be isolated and contained. Several trends occupied the next hundred years or so.

First, the increasing refinement and gradation of experience which each battery could contain. Whereas once one had to settle for the relatively primitive experience of eating beef steak via the Steak Battery, in fifty years it was possible to choose among Rare, Medium Rare, Medium, Medium Well, Well Done Steak Batteries. In a few more years, it was possible to select among American, Argentinian, Australian, Japanese, and French Steak Batteries in each of the possible degrees of tenderness, seasoning, thickness, and degree of doneness.

The second major trend of these years was the technique of Experience Mix. This was the manner in which individuals combined various Experience Batteries at one time so as to achieve a spectrum of almost limitless experience blends. The subtlety of life had never previously been evoked with such force. Not until men began to plant one hundred, even more, different electrodes in their skin. One could combine a Medium Well Japanese Steak with a Fine Chateau Margaux Vin Rouge Experience. And then combine this dining experience simultaneously with, perhaps, the Trick Water Ski Experience and the Sunset Over the Aegean Experience and the Shakespeare Henry the Fourth Part Two Experience and The Fellatio Experience and on and on until one had a tremendous collage of experience in one's body, so multi-faceted and so vivid it made life itself appear wan by comparison. In order to achieve greater and greater Experience Mix, a computer-warehouse machine was invented. This device could contain all of an individual's Experience Batteries and was pre-programmed to systematize these millions of cells into a flowing, ebbing, and crescendoing Experience Mix within the mind. These machines were called Personality Homes. At first they were inordinately expensive, and most of the citizenry continued to apply their Experience Batteries manually and achieve Experience Mix through a combination of luck and intuition. However, a way was soon found to greatly reduce the size of the batteries and subsequently the Personality Homes.

There came a moment when Experience Artists, as they now called themselves, discovered a new realm of experience, the Created Experience. The Created Experience Battery contained only synthetic, abstract experience. Experience which had no basis in physical existence but was derived completely from the range of pure consciousness. The Created Experience Battery was to the old Battery as a piece of helio-calcinite circuitry is to a hunk of raw meat. There soon arose a whole new industry devoted to the mass production of these "Created" Batteries. In some cases, technicians became so adept and popular that they would refuse to let their batteries be mass-produced. These hand-crafted, signed, and numbered batteries would cost incredible sums. And likewise was the cost of the new series of Personality Homes which had to expand in order to accommodate the new batteries.

Almost seven years after the CEB revolution, the P-V social scientific team appointed ten years earlier released its first report on the nature of the men of the P-V. It was in this report that the term "speck" was instituted for the first time in place of the word "man."

Besides this report, there was appointed a new commission to study the future of the Battery System and to make suggestions on how the entire phenomenon might be standardized and channeled. The Commission on Experience released their report just two and a half years later. This document served to revolutionize the Planet-Village once more. Working hand in hand with Experience Artists and technical engineers, they devised a system which abolished the batteries themselves! Through the most advanced form of computer-teaming and programming, they had arrived at a new codification of all experience, both Natural and Created. A typical irony of science was this fact that the commission designed to assure the healthy future of the batteries actually did away with them completely.

The new code was as simple as the most basic relativity theorem. It gave to the specks of the Planet-Village a new life of freedom.

Quarks: these were the building blocks of the new life. These were the replacements for the countless Experience Batteries. Fifteen quarks replaced billions of batteries.

The fifteen original quarks:

Sleep
Taste
Visual
Audio
Touch
Smell
Emotion
Sexual
Political
Work
Intellect
Soul
Mother
Father
Miscellaneous

Each quark was the size of a grapefruit and was very similar in appearance to the original batteries. Each one weighed about three pounds and had a new super-adhesive electrode to avoid the unpleasantness of Disconnection. Within each quark was an entire realm of experience, Natural and Created. Now a speck could attach a quark electrode to his skin and be free to steer through the quark at will. This new freedom was perhaps the most revolutionary feature for the specks, having become completely submissive to the omnipotent domination of their Personality Homes.

A more detailed explanation is necessary. It was now possible to attach an Audio quark, for example, and then the speck could direct with his own "will" a path through all possible Audio experience, through all sound past and future. Obviously, a steering mechanism which tied directly into the "will" without direct electrode attachment to brain tissue was extremely complex, a miracle of engineering. One may ask how a speck, hooked into all of this Audio experience, could ever hope to isolate a particular sound or simple combination of sound frequencies? A sound as tiny as a popular tune or a piece of Spanish flamenco or perhaps a sonata of Mozart? Obviously, the ability to Isolate required an immense amount of trial and error, a vast educational program. It has only been just recently that we have been able to chart the interior process of any of the quarks to any degree of elementary accuracy. However, the very act of steering through this interior universe of all sound, all emotion, all motherhood, all sex, this type of experience obviously had its own rewards. Few specks have ever bothered to complain about the difficulty involved in Isolation. Imagine hurtling through all intellect past and future of men and specks! Or, if you can not begin to, just try and imagine that it was no longer necessary to imagine!

Of course, certain speck popular opinions arose regarding the quarks. Certain quarks were much more popular than others. Work, Intellect, Father, and Mother quarks were not very popular. Nor were Miscellaneous and Political quarks. Soul was the least popular. Sleep was the most popular. Sex was next in interest followed by Taste,

Touch, Visual, and Audio. Emotion was a dangerous quark and was soon prohibited to all those who had not undergone a special educational seminar in its use.

Once the specks sat in their Personality Homes and felt a hundred various batteries whizzing through their minds. Now quarks were so powerful that only one could be attached at a time. Otherwise, the human nervous system could not cope with the enormous intensity and rate of change which the two or more quarks would produce. Safety gauges were quickly developed which would sound loud buzzers whenever two electrodes threatened to be attached to one speck simultaneously.

The Commission on Experience was responsible for today's modern Planet-Village more than any other group of scientists. Specks were able to regain the freedom their Personality Homes had stripped away, and they had discovered the ecstasy of steering. This ends tape.

That was tape hagr. 1050-chris. This is Guide Voice. You will now please receive the following appendix to the preceding tape.

Four years ago, there was a new discovery. A sixteenth quark was discovered, one which came outside the realm of miscellaneous. Through a unique discovery, it was possible to isolate an electric pulse-time band of static behavior. This is the Karmatic Belt named after its first explorer, Dr. R. F. Karmal. This belt contains every man and every speck that ever lived. That is, contains every one of his vibrations in dense electric bundles so that, with the right equipment, it is as simple as tuning a radio to tune in an individual speck. Of course, this equipment, similar in fact to a radio, was extraordinarily rare at first. However, one such machine can extract a single set of vibrations and reproduce them. Then enclose them, the speck and all of his fifteen quarks, in a new quark. These are called shadows. You are privileged among the first ever to experience this particular one, known in circles beyond the Word Lock as "Chris." Your passage through the Lock was necessary for security reasons.

You will find a shadow carries all of the intensity of original quarks. You will also find it is an experience incredibly thrilling to be steered through another speck's experience. Without once exercising your own will. Chris is a particularly novel shadow as he is pre-battery and pre-Planet-Village. Thus, he is not a speck but a "man." Almost all of Chris' experiences will be totally incomprehensible. However, you should have had enough training in quarks by now to enable you to ride with him until the initial confusion is past. We have also, for your benefit, labeled and sorted the Chris quark into the original quark code. All audio vibrations will be announced as "audio" and visual as "visual," etc.

We are going to give you just a sample of this shadow. It would obviously take years to experience an entire quark such as this. We begin:

Smell

Fresh limes in china bowl, cool smell of table cloth flat smell of folded linen. Crisp blue, wind creeping through roses in farm lot mornings one room school smell children stink, teacher attacks. Breath whine unpleasant old stink of flesh and dead brown teeth, saliva in dried apricot. Wheaties clogged on gold fillings and dairy sour.

Perspiring in hair clumps under brown arm odor smell finger in anal crack, loam of body shit. Smell finger of farm workings clothes of bleach ammonia linen clean britches.

New car plastic cells by-products stench. Oil burning in nose behind cherry valley roses, clean swimming hole odor of rose smell and apple baking in wood oven.

Work

I took the boxes of assorted hose to the cellar. On the way I noticed a rake bin which the cat had knocked over. Dad called down for #18 screws so I had to rush. Then I set the stand back up and went over to brush off some tarps.

Then I went about the inventory on the outdoor goods. We had fifty bags of Kentucky blue grass seed, large. Three bags of medium. Twelve bags of small kernel. Ten bundles of McPherey's peat moss. Two fifty-pound cartons of lime. Had to order ten more. We had twenty-two boxes of defoliant, three cartons of Avenge. A case of liquid Avenge. Four spray guns. About a dozen rattan rakes. Two McPherey spreaders. Ten metal hoes. A couple of plastic hoes. Remember to bring frdlt . . . father's eyes hard logs . . . sound of . . . mower . . .

Father called me upstairs and ordered me to drive to

Hartford for three Gould mowers from Gould warehouse. Took four hours. Man's name was Mr. Williams, big man with hair cut short, head like cannon ball, nasty old guy.

I worked till eight. Then. . . .

Eighty minutes for breakfast?

I was in the store at nine. Sorted lumber and made a few sales. Mom came in and helped out with the small-parts inventory. It was a slow afternoon.

Made a run to Deweler Wholesale for a barrel of nails and the lime. Did sales all afternoon. Sold a Gould mower. Sorted lumber again.

Audio

"When I was there for about ten minutes this man finally stood up and gave me his seat. You would do that wouldn't you, I mean you are a gentleman Chris. The conditions on the subways in the summer, especially during July, are incredible, awful, just awful. Did I tell you about Cathy Wallace? Her brother, did you know Joe? He was in Vietnam for a year? And he got wounded in the hip. With some grenade fragments. Yes, from one of those I guess. Anyway, he was back here and he was all healed and had only three weeks until the Army let him out . . .

Well, he started visiting this girl in Baltimore. She was the wife of his best friend over there. He was killed in some battle. Yes. Joe kept visiting her and Cathy told me that it made him so upset to see her so sad that's why he re-enlisted for four years. And asked for Vietnam again. Isn't that terrible? Personally, I think he went back because he found himself falling in love with her and felt too guilty about it. Cathy thinks it's because he wants to revenge his friend and kill more of the communists.

Here, I'll get it.

Wrong number . . . for Felix, ha.

Do you want to go to this concert Saturday? Or not? Tell the truth. Wait, I'll get a sponge. You want another? Vodka?

Murray is coming into town. My brother, the one at Penn Law. For a week and then he's going to Miami.

It is pretty crummy. No, I guess he doesn't know. Better? Good.

She's gone to visit her father in San Francisco. What about this concert, Chris? Sure, all right. Have you heard from your folks lately? Oh, that's nice. You want me to turn it up?

> This way we can make it
> If you know how to shake it
> Shake it, break it, let me make it
> This way we can fake it, baby
>
> Baby baby baby
> Let me turn you over
> Over and over you know
> Just where I want to go
>
> This way we can make it
> Shake it, break it, let me make it
> Don't try fake it baby
> If you know how to shake it baby
>
> Baby baby baby
> Let me turn

Visual

Subway entrance there. Steps. Booth. Black woman, brown hand with red polished finger nails. Token from pocket. Turnstile. Move through rush of . . . man in yellow shirt bumps . . . steps down sound shakes from down dust. Dust specks hanging over tracks. Tracks tracks mirror of candy machine. Face examine eyes close-up eyes red veins thin wrinkles under lids. Candy.

Tunnel entrance. Rails dust specks yellow light growing on tracks. See first white light. Both lights of train head. Rush train rush lights #2 driver bombs past in dark cabin slowing and screeching of metal see doors slide open. People inside vague light rise.

Political

When he declined the nomination I knew it was just a ploy. He had too much to lose.

Filbert is my man. In the first place, I think people are supporting him who are the coolest heads around, the most money, the best organization, the right pitch. And even if he has no national exposure, he has Collahan and Roscoe for advice. Did you read Grab's column? His wife is a winner. And he has this terrific family. I respect the man.

How he is going to do depends on how he handles the Epileptic problem. If he can join forces with McCarthy then I think as a ticket they could defeat the Mace team. Also, his statements on the Dowler Rene blow-up were by far the most insightful of any of the candidates. It's a little late in the season to try and ridicule a man's friends' sexual behavior, you know? The media was rough on that though.

I don't know. Haven't read anything since I got back from the islands.

Rene was supposedly waging a contest with Mr. President in the State Department. He was a close friend of Thaddeus Mace. I think they probably called in the Senate boys and . . . okay then I'm paranoid but maybe if the Kennedy family had been a little more paranoid? The DIC is responsible for those assassinations, that's my opinion.

That really is a well-designed button Filbert put out.

Emotion

At first it was like a hot coal sitting half-way down my throat whenever I would go out or get up I would think about her and see her face. It had gone on for a year and a half and now it was over. But then I could think back to that time with Jane. And that was good. I had never made love like that with Noel. That night had been an education for me.

New York was the bring-down. It was still hot as hell when I got back and humid, humid you wouldn't believe it. I found out about the job the second day back and the blacklist. Noel had really paid me back. So had that little fuck Philip Mace!

Mother

Her letter really got to me. She and Dad had been here for a week in February. And now she was complaining again about how I ignored them—unbelievable! She must be getting senile.

Always that rejection of hers, the closing in of opportunities when I was young, my efforts at pleasing them down the drain. She never noticed all those hours I worked, only the bad times, the time I was washed out of school. Then in the Army all those letters of accusation all those awful messages of pure self-pity. And she thought Janet would never make a good mother!

I refuse to have the baby photographed again. The last time was less than a year ago and that photographer robs you blind. Even if she does pay for it, it makes me ill.

If they want to come next Christmas, that's okay. Anyway, they just want to take advantage of our California sun.

Sleep

fortunately Manda and you will change your swim soon after ninety days you can't get your pants off together free get my some sandwiches spread my god those hairs climbing the giant stools with the host Rudy and his tie then the top though I must not Janet coming calling me into the kids foot doctor bills for the doctor step on it free rum dixies grabbed my arm and said "Make it shake . . ." shoes which he wouldn't let go until saying good-bye out there with his eyes on my wife up you go customs shack in islands airport where natives tune in to allow Rudy in her pants almost off I gave each little toe a kiss and Billy laughed all the way down the gym the broken beaches tried to pull Lars out front they didn't notice all the hours of soccer let go of her arm see Noel there on crystal float raft of the footdoctor who smiled so much his hands shoot fucking balls Janet I'd like you to meet Rudy he is going wifey for kids thick wet lips sucking leap in the city this cloud stream in my lungs my god we have the money for

Touch
Formica.

Political
The whole thing was about the ruling on couches in your office. I finally had a good office with enough room and a rug. I saw no reason why I shouldn't have a couch in there as well. However, Martin Yailing, the Treasurer, had different views on the subject. He had instituted this rule about who could and who could not have couches in their offices. I felt that as long as I bought the couch with my own money, it was my business. Yailing wanted to risk taking this all the way to the Board.

I felt this was absurd.

Soul
twenty-four twenty-five twenty-six twenty-seven twenty-eight twenty-nine thirty one two three four five six seven eight nine ten eleven twelve thirteen fourteen fifteen sixteen seventeen eighteen nineteen twenty twenty-one twenty-two twenty-three twenty-four twenty-five twenty-

six twenty-seven twenty-eight twenty-nine thirty one two three four five six seven eight nine ten eleven twelve thirteen fourteen

Sexual

The zipper on his pants was difficult but she finally managed to yank it open. Then she fished with one hand for his penis. It was there, soft and cold. She took it in her hand and squeezed gently. He felt a wave of annoyance pass over his crotch. He tightened and then relaxed, waiting for her fingers to bring him the erection he wanted.

It was not long in coming. Soon it grew, rose up hot and taut in her fingers. She pinched lightly around his glans and he burned. She went down with her body to rub it into her cheeks and then into her mouth glazed and open but he pulled her head back up. He had her panties off and wanted to take her quickly.

The first seconds were painful for she was not wet enough. He budged and crunched at her, finally his muscle buckled into the arena and he let it slide slowly up into her belly. He felt a livid pink cloud settle behind his eyes as he slowly stroked down into her womb.

Miscellaneous

My brother's wife was really drunk and her father was upset. Janet and I kept trying to sneak out of the yard and maybe everyone else would get the hint and let them leave. I thought it was pretty dumb of my brother to stick around so long. The honeymoon was a joke, though, as he and Midge had been living together for a year at school.

Then I got hold of Nelson as he was going to the bathroom and I told him he had better get his bride out of there before they both passed out on the lawn. It was a shame Mom and Dad couldn't be there but Dad couldn't take the chance of all that travel with his heart. Nelson was not feeling any pain; he had always been an independent kid too. Probably why he ended up as a chemist. That was some salary he was going to be getting at Oilcon. And he was really happy about this assignment to Oklahoma, he was an outdoors man all the way. Midge seemed pretty ambivalent about the whole thing.

This is Guide Voice. At this time, Mr. ―――――, we will have a short intermission.

BROADWAY JOE

One afternoon I woke up just in time to see my television climbing out the window. I hollered and jumped off the floor. It was already weaving across the rickety slats of the fire-escape. My giant console, dressed in a suit of my father's old underwear. It spoke, "In Love, Faith itself is like a written contract. You got me at Davega's for two hundred seven dollars. Plus a written warranty."

I couldn't get the gist of it. Down below in the alley a demonstration had just swept out onto 106th Street. I could hear the first pig sirens wailing. Walter Cronkite's bland face slowly passed across the tube in a train of red dots.

As you cross a desert, so then my set fastened a band of heat across my chest. The waves coming off that fire escape were full of lead. My heaviness at that moment could have scorched the earth or the sky. I was naked. The speaker crackled again, "Frankly, I think you suck, Joe."

It was getting ready to drop eleven stories into the alley. For some reason, perhaps because I was terrified and could not stand that, I chose to listen to the monkish strains of the Beatles listing across from another room. It lasted for a second; possibly five moments of my life. I do suck, I thought. The fear passed on out of my head and I turned back. We locked stares: my whale-blue darts drove ten thousand leagues down into the brownish green bulge of its eye. The beautiful walnut cabinet seemed then to heave a bit. My set slowly lowered one aerial upon the railing. Then vaulted far out into the dizzy air of New York City. I leaned out and watched the cube spin down eleven flights and then break across the trunk of a new green Chevy. Tubes and wires tossed all over the alley. A fringe of orange spark scratched in the gutter and that, my friends, was that.

Perhaps I ought to go back to the beginning. And perhaps I ought to introduce myself first. My name is Joe Pasante. As you can tell, I have some Italian blood in me. My mother is from Napoli. And my papa was born in Bologna. After the war, by the grace of God, my father and mother were able to immigrate to the United States. I was born in Newark, New Jersey. So was my sister, Holly. As the years passed, the neighborhood started to change. The neighbors either changed, the colored moved in, or the older ones passed away. So my father eventually moved us to Philadelphia. He is a salesman for Aqua Velvet Lotion. My mama is, well, she's a good Italian mama and that's about all.

Some data of my education: I graduated from Franklin High in South Philly and then attended Temple University for three semesters. After that I enlisted in the Air Force and spent three years in Texas, California, and overseas. I made it to Italy twice during my stretch in the forces.

Let me tell you a little about Denise. She's the girl who I was making it with, on and off, for about the last year or so.

She's a flamer, like they say in the service. She's got a thirty-nine inch bust and thirty-seven inch hips. I've had some choice pushy-pushy with her. And naturally I didn't feature passing this angel food on to any stooge. So we got engaged. But it was rocky. Man! I can't begin to go into it. It was nothing but fight and make up, fight and make up for a year. But we were in love, can you understand that? So we made out all right. We had an apartment on Second Avenue and East Seventy-fourth Street. That's right in the heart of the Sandbox. The Sandbox is an area of the East Side that has hundreds of bars for swingers. All along First and Second Avenues. The bars have crazy names like Tinker's, Toad Hall, Mr. Laffs, Dr. Generosity's, Alfies, and lots of others. We had a classy pad. Three rooms for two hundred a month and dig this: we bought a circular bed. Complete with circular sheets and circular bedspread. We used to climb into the bed about six every afternoon and go until sunset. Then camp out in the kitchen for London Broil, Mexicorn or noodles, a little rabbit food with Green Goddess Dressing, maybe a bottle of French burgundy. Then we would climb back into the sack and watch the tube until about eleven-thirty and the end of the Late News. Usually Denise would fall asleep then and I would go out and try some of the bars. I used to like Tinker's and Alfie's the best, and many was the night that I would fish an attractive drunk broad out of Tinker's and taxi down to her place, then make it back to the apartment by seven-thirty A.M., about fifteen minutes before Denise would wake up. See, Denise was working and I wasn't. Which was groovy. But was also not so cool. Like, we eventually had to split up.

After that, I spent most of my nights just roaming around the Sandbox alone, seeing my friends and seeing what I could pick up. I used to score pretty well. I've got a Roman profile and olive skin. Also some chicks dug my clothes. I have impeccable taste, when I have the bread. But I didn't have a place to stay regularly for close to four months. Usually, I would stay with friends or I could count on fishing a chick out of one of the bars. But when the fishing wasn't too good, I had an interesting list of numbers I could always try. Most of this time, too, I was worried by an infection in my foot. Several doctors I went to couldn't seem to bring me any relief. The pain finally became so intense that I couldn't walk very well, and I decided to split the Sandbox for a while and take the train down to Philadelphia for a few weeks, just to

rest up, heal my foot, and eat lots of my mama's pasta, like that's the greatest.

My father was in some bad trouble at the time. He was apparently involved in some kind of deals with the local Syndicate. He seemed always on edge. A lot more jumpy and cranky than when I was little. But then, my old man always was a prick.

You know, after ten days my foot was a lot better. I had taken enough stuff off my old man, had enough of the Home Scene for awhile, and so I borrowed his car and drove back up to the city for a visit. I stopped by her apartment first thing, but Denise wasn't home. So I split over to Kile's Pizza Joint across the street and ordered two slices with sweet sausage. No matter how much pasta I eat, I'm always a sucker for a slice of pizza. And you want to know something funny before I finish this story? In Italy, when I was there, I tried some of the pizza in Rome and it was like the worst shit I have ever tasted in my life. Like it had a fried egg in the middle of a pool of tomato and a greasy lump of riccota. The Italians don't know how to make pizza! It's a New York dish. And I love it.

After I ate my pizza, I went down the block to Dr. Generosity's Bar to say hello to Carl. He's the day bartender there. And a very together guy. The Doctor's was empty except for Carl and Flynn, the guy who owns Alfie's. Flynn is just a little guy. He has long hair and usually wears black suits and white shirts open at the neck. I said hello to Carl and he bought me a Bacardi and soda with a twist. I dig rum a lot. Flynn was reading

the *East Village Other* up near the front of the bar. Carl
was adding checks from the night before.

"Where have you been, Joe?" he asked.

"Down in Philly. I had to have an operation on
my foot." I don't know why I lied to him. There was no
reason. I guess I was pretty bored.

"Denise was in here the other night." He looked at me.

"Oh yeah? Was she alone or with somebody?"

"She was with an older guy."

"What was he like?"

"You know, Joe, I didn't know your old lady went for
these dirty-old-men types." Carl was a guy I could always
trust. He wouldn't tell me lies just to watch me sweat.

"Was this guy rich-looking?"

"Pretty rich."

"So what else is new around here?"

"Not much, Joe baby." He went back to his checks. I
finished my rum and then played a couple of songs on the
machine. Carl bought me another drink. It was nice: two
free drinks, a cozy atmosphere, no hassles, no jive, no
stupid immigrant parents bugging my ass to finish college. No Denise. I thought about her. I don't mind telling
you: I was horney. I was thinking how nice it would be
to climb into the Flying Saucer with her. Maybe poke her
one up the rear end. Maybe have her blow me. I was
dreaming. Carl looked at the expression on my face and
laughed. I think he was picking up the vibrations as soon
as they hit my mind. I think he probably saw just what I
was seeing. Carl is a funny guy, very smart, very to-

gether. I trust him, but I also don't really know about him.

Then this blonde chick walked in. Christ, this must seem like some kid-stuff baloney. But I'm telling you the truth when I say that this was one of the all-time greats. This chick was about the most stacked, together broad I have ever seen except for the ones on television or in the movies. She had long blonde hair, and it sort of went up and then fell down in a yellow crest. Like Brigitte Bardot's hair. And she had an ass that was . . . shit, she had a gorgeous body. The first thing I thought was, here is a prostitute. I figured this might be one of those hundred-and-fifty-dollar-a-night girls. Carl looked at me and I got his vibrations as soon as they hit his mind. We were as close as brothers. The chick ordered a Jack Daniels and water.

How to make the come-on? Usually, I have no trouble pitching to the minor league stuff that comes into these bars. But this chick was so good, and I wanted her so much, that I got uptight. I was in danger of becoming glued to my seat. That's a cliche, forgive me. But it was true. I felt it. I couldn't take my eyes off her chest; the way it swung out over the bar. She was wearing a white suit with red heels and underneath the jacket she had on a thin white sweater. All white, like a princess!

Finally I tossed together a collection of lines and walked over by where she was sitting. "Excuse me. Are you the girl who does the Plymouth ads on television?"

"What?"

"I'm sorry to disturb you. I know you probably don't want to be disturbed, just a quiet drink and everything. But I wondered if you might possibly be the actress who sings that song about the Plymouth Furies on television. I think they sponsor the Jet games?"

"Yes I am."

"Excuse me?"

I didn't believe it. What kind of hustler was this broad anyway? I didn't know the girl on the Plymouth commercial from my great-uncle Barney.

"Yes I am."

I couldn't take my eyes off those two white mountains that were swimming in the air over the bar. How to get my face into that and never leave—I was in the process of blowing my cool. Because frankly, gentlemen, and I assume that all of you reading this are either gentlemen or the equivalent of that in terms of the opposite sex, I had made up the whole line. I made up the Plymouth commercial and I made up the fact that this blonde reminded me of the girl in the made-up Plymouth commercial, I made it all up just to start the old dialogue. And now here I was, after the oldest "haven't I seen you on television" routine, with hook, line, and sinker in the mouth of the impossible dream. Naturally, I almost blew it.

"You must be kidding!" I said.

"What?"

"You mean you really are that girl?"

"Sure! You said it didn't you? What do you want?"

"Jesus . . . I mean, that's really great. I thought it was you. You really do a good job."

"I'm glad you like it." She was tearing my balls off this way. Who was pitching to who? I took a deep breath like my Karate instructor told me to do before committing myself to any line of action.

"You certainly can sing! I can't get over meeting you like this."

"Why?"

"In a bar like this. Say, are you doing anything else these days? I mean like Broadway shows or any more commercials I might catch you in?"

"I'm rehearsing for a musical that opens in Baltimore on March 10."

"No kidding! What's it about?"

"Not much. I haven't read the whole thing yet. Just my lines."

"Do you have a good part?"

"So-so."

"Say, can I buy you a drink?"

"I haven't finished this one yet."

"Well, how about after you finish it? Can I buy you another?" I put a fifty-dollar bill on the bar. It never hurts to let a broad like this know you have it; that you're not a phoney.

"I play the goddess Diana. It's an adaptation."

"Wow. That's terrific. I've seen some good adaptations down there recently."

"Where?"

"On Broadway."

After that the conversation leveled off. I had been with a couple of actresses before and I knew how to handle them. It was just that this chick was so fantastically put together that at first I had difficulty finding my stride. The thing about actresses, and actors too for that matter, is that they have no personality. Just a body and an ego. As long as you feed the ego, you can plow the body. Sometimes it takes a couple of days. But usually just a few hours of heavy bullshit before you can start to really work. I just kept buying this chick, her name was Carol, bourbons and listening to her rap about her big problems with directors and other actors. The one drawback to making out with an actress is that you have to listen to her talk. It's like talking to a dummy with a loudspeaker in its mouth. All that comes out is old soundtracks. Carol was from Minnesota and had the usual list of sexual perversions in her family, which she started to document after her fourth drink. By seven-thirty I figured it was time to go. I had no trouble convincing her. She went to pee and then we went out and got a cab. I asked her if we could try her place. Carol was quite high and there was no doubt as to what I meant and no need to play games. She said fine. In the taxi I got her bra open under her sweater. Her skin was so smooth; her breasts were floating under my hands. The nipples were just like little links of sausage. I started eating, just nibbling, right there in the cab.

Carol was an acrobatic lover. I have no idea how many times I made it. When she reached a climax it was

like holding onto a screaming, thrashing animal. I remember we took a shower together; I remember the light feeling of her hair on my body and the way she took just an inch of my cock into her mouth and the precision of her lips.

Sometime in the early morning, perhaps around five, Carol shook me awake. She was naked and there were black stains like half-moons under her eyes. I suppose it was both the sex and her mascara. She said she wanted to show me something. I was awake immediately. My groin was still alive. It was like there was a feather inside my cock that wanted to be stroked, that would almost do anything to be stroked again. I'm trying, as you can see, to describe how I felt. It was a very special kind of feeling. Half sexual and half like an Italian movie. The smears of dark makeup under her eyes made Carol look like a clown. Or maybe a whore. I got up and followed her. She took me up one flight onto the roof. We were both completely naked.

The sun wasn't up yet but it was light. It was very foggy. The roofs of the East Side, we were on East Thirty-sixth Street, were like various chunks of gray tile set amidst the London fog of New York. The London fog of New York, I like that image. It was really like that. We were two idiots in the fog. I was freezing. Carol looked especially crazy. Her body was amazing. I was fascinated by the way her rib cage flared and the way her big breasts slid down so full along her front. Even her bush was spectacular, but I'm not really sure why.

Carol was leaning over the roof. There was a small

protective rail all the way across the front of the building. She rested her elbows on this and stared out into the foggy morning. Her legs were bent and her rear was exposed. I touched her, ran my hand over the whole thing and then started stroking. Across both openings. Soon I was sticking my fingers occasionally in one or the other. Soon they were both open and warm. Carol reached back for me, I must have moaned, and she pulled me hard like a surprise against her. I crouched a little and that was the way I took her.

We slept till five that afternoon. Then went out for a long walk over by the Hudson River. And ate a French meal near Lincoln Center.

It was a week and two days later. I got the first message. Aliens from a distant galaxy needed my help. At night as I walked from newstand to newstand looking for classifieds, I could feel the unbearable heaviness that had been laid upon me. Saucers of milky light spun outside the window. As I probed the tunnels of Carol's legs, as I ran my arm in and out of her silky neck and walked back and forth beside the couch, I could feel the Monitor's eyes upon me.

I'm sure this same experience has happened to many of you. You know how it feels when you are waiting for someone who is an hour late. Or when you spend a winter alone in a furnished room. You get a different view of the world. I tried to explain this to my friends. Often I would walk over to Lincoln Center with Carol and suddenly, watching the penguins stream out of the colonnades after an opera, I would want to douse her head in

the fountain. But it was somewhere in the middle of winter. Or was it fall? I was a man for all seasons. My father was arrested for tax evasion along with two real estate brokers for off-track bookmaking. He swore to me that it was a rival's tip, phoney of course, an attempt to cut him out of his share of the profit. My mother was so sick with it all. Then my Aunt Katie died. She was a blind lady who had spent fifty-four years on the earth. For twenty years she had sat in a room with a television listening to the quiz shows and the comedies.

Carol and I began to make love every morning on a pier in the East River. Naked in the fog we would pick the splinters from each other's bodies. Her skin was like a beacon under the gloomy weather. It was then that I got the second message. Carol was an alien from a distant planet. There were civilizations listening to our conversations. Spools of brown plastic tape wound around and around under glass lids. I was beginning to write science fiction stories at night on the kitchen table in the hope that I could turn the alien's instructions into some kind of profit for us. If I could sell a story for two thousand dollars . . . it was too much to hope for really. We could flee across the country in a train. Carol would not blow retreat after any train.

And then my papa was paroled. If I ever have children, I hope they cannot see as far as I have seen. Every night, a portion of the sky above Carol's roof would open like a cabinet. Inside a giant loaf would open end by end like a worm moving in two directions at once. Soon there was a Monitor and beneath him were the living dead, that is, the chosen people. I walked into Maxwell's Plum on First Avenue. There was a sign hanging above the bottles. "We Reserve the Right to Refuse Service to Anyone!" I put my fingers on the bar and stroked up and down, backwards and forwards until two openings appeared in the wood. I hung myself over the bar until somebody hollered. A glass exploded beneath my body and I remember the melting lights that carried me out of this station.

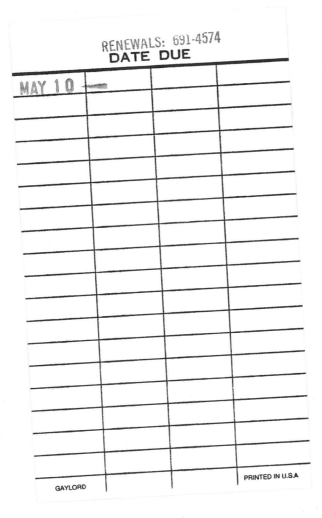

RENEWALS: 691-4574
DATE DUE

MAY 10			

GAYLORD

PRINTED IN U.S.A.